J[...] [...]ope you enjoy this book. [...]
read, [...]
upstate New Y[...], Sa[...]a [...]nd th[...] Virgin islands. [...]he graduated
from St Peter and Paul High School in St Thomas and moved to
NYC where she modelled for five years for Elite. She went to France
and met her husband at the polo club. All that is true. But she mostly
likes to make up stories.

Praise for Jennifer Macaire's *Time For Alexander* Series

'A fascinating glimpse into the Ancient World jam-packed
with adventure and colour.' **Jodi Taylor**, author of
the best-selling *Chronicles of St Mary's* series

'A vividly written, characterful, informed and unusual
take on Alexander and Ancient Times. I loved it.'
Carol McGrath, author of *The Silken Rose*

'Fun, sexy and at times incredibly sad, the story held me to
the end and the research was incredible' **Karen King**

Also by Jennifer Macaire

Tempus U Series

A Remedy In Time
A Crown in Time

Time For Alexander Series

The Road to Alexander
Legends of Persia
Son of the Moon
Storms Over Babylon
Chants to Persephone
The Soul of Time
The Eternal Banquet

Horse Passages Series

Riders of the Lightning Storm
Lost Storm Rider
Rebel Storm Rider

Short Stories

The White Queen
Honey on your Skin

A REMEDY IN TIME

JENNIFER MACAIRE

ACCENT

First published in 2021
by HEADLINE ACCENT,
An imprint of HEADLINE PUBLISHING GROUP

2

Cataloguing in Publication Data is available from the British Library

ISBN 978 1 7861 5790 4

Typeset in 10.5/13pt Bembo Std by Jouve (UK), Milton Keynes

Printed and bound in Great Britain by Clays Ltd, Elcograf S.p.A.

MIX
Paper from
responsible sources
FSC® C104740

Headline's policy is to use papers that are natural, renewable and recyclable
products and made from wood grown in well-managed forests and other
controlled sources. The logging and manufacturing processes are expected
to conform to the environmental regulations of the country of origin.

HEADLINE PUBLISHING GROUP
An Hachette UK Company
Carmelite House
50 Victoria Embankment
London
EC4Y 0DZ

www.headline.co.uk
www.hachette.co.uk

A REMEDY
IN TIME

To my dogs, past and present. For every book I wrote, you were at my feet – patient, loving, (and sometimes very smelly, especially if you just came bouncing in from outside after rolling in something awful). If I could, I'd go back in time to see you all again: Hessie, the amazing babysitter; Fudge, the protector; Rusty, the best buddy; and Auguste, who now, at 15, is blind, deaf, but not dumb (he barks at me when he thinks it's time to eat): best dog ever. The neighbours all greet him with enthusiasm when we're out for a walk – and then, as an afterthought, add, 'Oh, and hi, Jenny'.

Glossary

Some Chinese swear words

bèn dàn: a 'stupid egg', this term is used to call someone a fool/idiot/moron/etc.

wang ba: this can be translated roughly as 'bastard'.

wocao (or wo cao): 'Holy shit!', alternatively, 'fucking awesome!'

sha bi: cunt

ta ma de: the English equivalent of 'fuck', 'shit', or 'damn it'.

Some French swear words

merde: shit, damn — used extensively and for every frustrating situation

con, conne: stupid, cunt

putain(e): literally a whore, but can mean anything from 'shit' or 'shitty', to 'incredible' or even 'awesome'.

Yah's vocabulary

Makii: wolf

Nashdotso: smilodon

Shika: help

Shissi: sorry

Ahoh: yes

Ee: small, young

Adeez: family

Aki: where

Ako: this place/here

Some technology

Comlink – the comlink is the base for all the wearable technology, including the vitapak. It is usually worn on the wrist and can look like a small watch. Watches are obsolete – we all use comlinks. They also tell time and have calendars and agendas. You can wear the comlink like a bracelet, a ring, a necklace, or even implant it in your skin somewhere. The coolest ones are super-flat, are worn under the skin, and can imitate any tattoo design you want. The comlink communicates with all the technologies you use, including the floating screen.

Vidcam (also referred to as hovercam, since most of them fly) – records, photographs, communicates. Most are about the size of a hummingbird. The more sophisticated ones are the size of a fly. You program them and control them with your comlink, and you see the pictures they take on your floating screen.

Floating screen – A projected 3-D image from a vidcam that floats in the air. The screen can be transmitted via comlink. The vidcam doing the filming can be many kilometres away from its floating screen.

Vitapak – also called health packs, also called blood suckers. Handy things that give medicine, cut, cauterize, diagnose, X-ray – well, some do all those things. Like most healthcare, the vitapak's performance depends on how much you can pay, and most people only have the basic vitapak, which only takes your blood pressure and temperature. The vitapak communicates and works with a medbot, which looks like a giant spider. The medbot has taken the place of human doctors and surgeons.

PART I

HAMLET:

Let us go in together,
And still your fingers on your lips, I pray.
The time is out of joint — O cursèd spite,
That ever I was born to set it right!
Nay, come, let's go together.

Shakespeare, *Hamlet*, Act 1, Scene 5, 186-190

PART I

Chapter One

'Fleas cause typhus. More precisely, cat and opossum fleas. But it's far easier to blame immigrants. After all, the main victims of typhus are the homeless, those living in squalor, and those who cannot escape the proximity of infected animals. So, point at the poor immigrant. After all, it would be economically impossible to control fleas, whereas if you stir up enough fear in the population towards immigrants, all you have to do is build a wall.'

~ Excerpt from '**Environmental risk and typhus in the late twentieth century**', Robin Johnson, Center for Environmental Biology and Ecosystem Studies, Tempus University, Berkeley, Western State of California, in *BMC Infectious Diseases Microbiology*. 3370 March 6; 30(3):204–208.

'The major clinical signs and symptoms of this new typhus (now referred to as Typhus-77) are disturbing: an acute and high fever, thrombocytopenia, leukopenia, elevated serum hepatic enzyme levels, gastrointestinal symptoms, and multiple organ failure, with a death rate of ~100%. It can infect animals as well as humans, and we suggest declaring this a national emergency in order to free funds to develop a vaccine as soon as possible. In the meantime, further clinical, epidemiologic, and laboratory research is needed to better understand the transmission dynamics of this pathogen, if possible, going back as far as possible in time to get samples.'

~ **Excerpt from a letter** from Professor Powell, Center for Environmental Biology and Ecosystem Studies, to the head of the Health Technology R&D Project of the Ministry of Health and Welfare, Anchorage, Western State of California. 22 December, 3377.

★

3

The following are notes from the dossier of Robin Johnson, presented to the Court of Time Travel and Technology. 1 May, 3378:

If I'm to tell everything about the trip back to time and its aftermath – the reason for the voyage, why I was chosen for the trip, and who got killed – I have to start at the beginning. As my boss, Dr Powell, would say: 'You have to know the background of anything before you can put it into context.' He was also fond of saying, 'If you precipitate matters you will not be precise.' That's a good saying – and one that I always remember, mostly because Dr Powell said it nearly every day. I will therefore take my time and explain everything fully.

I was a researcher for the Center for Environmental Biology and Ecosystem Studies at the Tempus University time travel lab. Just for the record, and because I am precise, I will state that Dr Powell was against my going back in time. Dr Powell and I had been working together for ten years, since I started my Masters programme. Dr Powell's wife told me, in the beginning, that no one had lasted more than six months working with him, but that I would surely learn a lot and should take the job anyhow. She had been doing the job interviews since his last (twelfth) assistant had quit and the department had decided that maybe Dr Powell shouldn't be doing his own hiring. He tended to take brilliant but sensitive students and proceed to demolish them. Mrs Powell thought that I would probably last a little longer than the others, since I don't take anything personally. She was astounded when I lasted a year, after two years she started referring to me as 'a wonder', and after ten years, I'd pretty much been adopted as their surrogate daughter. Dr Powell stopped ranting after about three years – seeing it didn't affect me – and started to take me to conferences. After five years, he promoted me from assistant to collaborator (not that it made a wink of difference in my salary or status at the university). Dr Powell and I spent every working day together, and to tell the truth, I admired him immensely, so when he yelled at me I'd simply agree with everything he said. He was right, I was wrong, and since I never argued, we got along fine.

My job consisted mainly of identifying environmental threats, but Dr Powell often lent me out to different programmes, which was

4

how I landed at the Page Museum helping with their studies of pathogens of sabre-toothed tigers. They went extinct very quickly, and the Center wanted me to identify, if possible, the reason. From there, my name came up for a time-travel program that centred around smilodons – it wasn't precisely my speciality, but there weren't any Tempus U scientists with much knowledge about smilodons at that time.

There was another, more pressing reason for the trip as well. A new disease resembling typhus, but not responding to any of the typhus treatments, had started to ravage the continent. As an environmental threat specialist, my thesis had been on typhus. I'd written so many papers on the subject that when the new sickness appeared I got flagged right away. What happened was I had a hypothesis that the disease came from the last ice age and was now making a comeback, aided by global warming. Several of the smilodon skulls had tested positive for this new disease, now called Typhus-77 because it was first identified in the year 3377. The symptoms and vectors were similar to typhus, but it was far more deadly and was viral, not bacterial.

When I was chosen for the program, Dr Powell begged me to reconsider. If he had put his foot down and told me I *couldn't* go, I would have listened. But being told to reconsider isn't the same thing as being forbidden. I reconsidered everything, and decided I'd still like to do it. I'd been watching historians and scientists go back in time for ten years now, and I admit, I was curious.

Tempus University has many lucrative time-travel programs, which is good – because time travel is incredibly expensive. Historians go back in time for 24 hours and take holograms and bring back recordings of famous people. Scientists go back for two weeks and bring back holograms, recordings, and samples. Mostly, the programs I work on are based on the medical and ecological, with a big part about studying the evolution of pathogens. We do a lot of viral and bacterial research and research on plants and animals, which is why, when we send scientists back, they go in pairs. They need a lot of equipment. It can be dangerous.

In January, I had just completed a study on the possible causes of extinction of the sabre-toothed tiger based on the many fossils found in the La Brea tar pits. Page Museum had donated most of the samples, and they had also put in a demand for a holo film to be shown at the museum as part of the exhibit. It was a fairly common demand – immersive holograms from the past was how Tempus University met most of its funding requirements. Tempus was picky about what jobs they would accept, but this passed the vetting process with no trouble. A holo film starring sabre-toothed tigers and perhaps some other extinct animals: dire wolves, giant sloths, and hopefully a mammoth. And I would go and gather samples.

Here's where it gets tricky. As the long Pleistocene Age drew to a close, many of the highly successful large mammals began to go extinct. Huge herds of bison, mastodons, mammoths, horses, giant deer, and camels had grazed in North America, and sabre-toothed tigers and dire wolves preyed upon them. Then, somewhere around 10,000 BCE, they all vanished.

The animals we wanted to observe lived until about twelve to thirteen thousand years ago. We could only go back roughly twelve thousand years. No matter how hard the Time Sender tried, they could never get past the barrier of twelve thousand years. It wasn't a clear-cut number, but every single time traveller sent back further than that disappeared without a trace. In the Americas, twelve thousand years ago, things were happening that would affect the entire continent. The Ice Age was finished, but a period of bitter cold had reappeared and, for some reason, large animals were going extinct at incredible rates.

Human beings appeared on the scene at this time too, but my speciality was flora and fauna – so I only had a vague idea of the different cultures that had migrated from Eurasia over the land bridges in the far north. Homo sapiens has not changed much anatomically over the last 120,000 years, but it has undergone a massive cultural evolution. To avoid culture shock and undue influence on the future, anyone sent back was absolutely forbidden to come into contact with Palaeolithic people, so our mission consisted of getting samples, filming the animals, and – most importantly – avoiding contact with other humans.

When Professor Daws, the head of Palaeolithic Time Travel Studies, suggested that I might like to take the trip back, I was astonished. But he and the Page Museum rep both felt I was just the person to collect the most samples in the least amount of time. Our trip, being one of the most risky because of the distance to the past, couldn't last more than a week. They needed someone who wouldn't get distracted by anything not related to the matter at hand. I'd be accompanied by another scientist whose job would be to work with me (of course) but also to film and direct the survival side of the mission because I hadn't completed all the survival courses for such a trip, which was another reason Dr Powell was so set against me going.

A certain number of survival courses were recommended even though most time travellers didn't qualify as survival experts. However, the further back in time you go, the more dangerous it can be. In our day, the animals around us have evolved alongside humans for such a long time that their actions are nearly always predictable. Humans have come to recognize what is a threat and what is not. But twelve thousand years ago, animals had just come into contact with humans and there were no set courses of action. When we see a wolf and it raises its hackles and snarls, we know it's threatening us. We back off. But it's taken thousands of years for wolves to be able to communicate with humans that way. We don't know that dire wolves had the same indications for threat. We don't even know how a sloth, or a camel, or a giant beaver would react upon coming face to face with a human.

Or how a sabre-toothed tiger would.

Chapter Two

23 January, 3378

'I'm not going back in time with her.'

The voice was low, but I heard, and I stopped to listen. Not very polite, but I recognized the speaker, and my skin prickled. *Donnell Urbano was in the dean's office – why?*

'Don't be—'

The dean's voice was cut off as Donnell interrupted.

'I'll be however the hell I want to be. In this case, I'm telling you right now, there is no way I'm going back in time with her. You can find someone else. That's my—'

Now it was his turn to get cut off. 'I will listen to your complaint in full, in two days' time, *after* you complete the first exercise together. Then you can express your misgivings and I will be more inclined to listen. Right now, you are basing your refusal on – what are you basing it on, by the way?'

Donnell gave an incredulous laugh, and I leaned closer to hear. 'You're kidding, right? Powell's protégé gets turned loose in the Palaeolithic and you're wondering why I'm worried? The girl has never been on a time trip before. She's untrained, untried, and frankly, I find her disconcerting. I've read her records. You can't cure dissociative amnesia. I'll give her one day. After that, find me a new partner.

I didn't stick around to hear any more. That *wang ba* wanted to get rid of me, but I wouldn't go without a fight. My past had nothing to do with who I was today. He was wrong, I *was* cured. I'd passed enough psychology tests to prove it. I turned around and headed towards the university's underground station. I was never above asking for help, and I knew just the person to give it to me. At the station, I got in the pod and chose the destination 'zoological park'. The doors slid shut and the pod shot through the tunnel while I slouched in my seat and fumed. Disconcerting? I'd show him disconcerting.

At the zoological park I jumped on the monorail and took it straight to the main office. My researcher pass gets me into places you wouldn't believe. This was one perk. I get to go to museums, zoos, greenhouses, laboratories, and gymnasiums for free. The gymnasiums are to encourage us to stay in shape. Nothing worse than a flabby scientist, says Dr Powell sternly. He's right. He's always right.

At the main office I flashed my pass at the receptionist and asked for Jake Powell. He's Dr Powell's son, and we've known each other since I started working with his father. The girl calling him on the floating screen looked at me with interest. 'Whom shall I say is calling?' she asked.

Whom, shall? I almost rolled my eyes. The latest fad was speaking in old-fashioned lingo with Chinese and French swear words mixed in. *Forsooth, bèn dàn.* 'Robin,' I said, and waited as the screen hovered over to me and Jake's image appeared. He saw me and waved.

'Be right there, Robin,' he said.

The girl's interest sharpened like a laser beam. I understood why. Jake is considered amazingly handsome by most all females. I think he's handsome too, of course, but I'm uninterested in him as a serious mate. For one thing, I know Jake too well. He's incapable of commitment. He's been engaged to the same on-and-off again fiancée for five years now. His on-and-off again fiancée, Helen, has more arguments for marriage than an encyclopedia of engagement quotes. She might be determined, but Jake's a master at dodging. As soon as she starts planning the ceremony, he finds an excuse to break up. Usually it's another woman.

When he walked in the room, he gave the receptionist a friendly wave that turned her cheeks scarlet, and gave me a big hug. Then he

9

tousled my hair, which he knows I don't like, and he asked me what I was doing there.

'I need your help. I have a survival course in two days and I must pass it with flying colours.'

His eyebrows rose, which they always did when he was surprised. 'Flying colours, eh? All right. Let's get some gear, and we'll hit the campsite.' He turned to the girl sitting behind her desk, pretending not to listen to us. 'Call me if I'm needed.' He took my arm. 'If you're talking in clichés, it must be serious. So tell me, what's going on?'

We headed to the glass walkway that led from the main offices to the centre of the park. 'I've been chosen to go back in time in order to make a wildlife film. It's a fairly straightforward mission. We set up camp near a site that is well known for attracting large animals. We stay out of sight and film as much of the flora and fauna that we can in a radius of ten kilometres. We avoid contact with people. We collect samples. We pack everything up, make sure we've left nothing behind, and take the tractor-beam back on the seventh day.'

'Sounds easy,' he agreed. 'Climate? Season? Terrain?'

'Cool and possibly rainy. Even snow is a possibility. We are aiming to be there in the early summer, hopefully we'll be able to film immature as well as mature species.'

'That's not what I asked, but all right. Early summer. Cool, chances of snow. Must be high elevation then, right?'

'No, we will be in California, but the climate was different back then. We think there was a small ice age resulting in either an impact from a meteorite or extreme volcanic activity in northern Europe.'

He frowned. 'Just how far back are you going?'

'Twelve thousand years.'

'Robin!' He sounded upset. 'What did my dad say?'

'He said he wanted me to reconsider. But I did, and I thought it would be a once-in-a-lifetime chance. So I told him. He said he'd hold my job for me. I think he was just making a joke, since I'm owed a year of vacation time, and he always said I could take it any time I wanted. I never had a vacation destination, but now I do. I want to see a sabre-toothed tiger, Jake. Wouldn't you?'

'*Wocao*, yes!' But he shook his head. 'I'd love to see one, but I'm not crazy. You are, Robin, if you think you can sneak up on a bunch of wild animals and just start filming. You have no idea what they are capable of, or what they can do.'

'That's why we have telephoto lenses on our vidcams. We won't get anywhere near them. We'll set up some motion sensors, put cameras around, send some vidcams into the air, and stay safe and sound in our treeblind or hide. When there are no animals around, we go out and gather samples. I'm not stupid. Look, are you going to help me or not?'

We stepped out of the walkway and found ourselves at the top of the stairs leading down to the savannah exhibit. Jake didn't give me any warning. With a vicious shove, he pushed me down the stairs. I didn't panic. I just had time to evaluate the angle of my descent so that I could land on my hands and break my fall, but I hit my shoulder on the wall harder than I would have liked. I ended up on my feet, about fifteen steps down from Jake. 'You always did fight dirty,' I told him.

His grin didn't reach his eyes. 'I haven't even started yet.'

That's another thing. Jake's an expert in self-defence and he's been training me since we met. I rubbed my shoulder. 'I'm not here about the survival part of the course. I don't know how to set up a campsite correctly.'

Jake led me into the park. 'Your survival is going to depend on your campsite. To set up your tent, first look for mostly level ground. It should be at least slightly higher than surrounding terrain, so rainwater drains away from instead of pooling around it. Try to find a spot free of rocks, roots, dead trees, and mammoth trails.'

'I'm not planning on camping on a mammoth trail,' I said.

He stopped and grabbed my arm. 'We're not playing anymore. You don't even know what a mammoth trail looks like. No one does. Just stay away from any area that is worn smooth from lots of traffic. Individual footprints may not show up. You are going to set up a camp that's going to be your only protection for seven days and nights. You'd better do it right. Stay away from water. Cook, eat, and store your food well away and preferably downwind from your campsite. And when I say well away, I mean it. Change your dining area each day. Don't eat after dark. Carry a stun gun, set it on high, and sleep with it under your pillow. If something happens and you lose your weapons, keep a fire lit at all times and put long branches into it that you can grab and toss at critters if they get too near. Don't bring anything that smells like food into the tent with you – I'm talking about lip balm, sunscreen, or toothpaste.'

'I nodded. 'Makes sense. Don't carry anything that has an odour, and bring some scent-block spray. Do you think modern sprays will work?'

'Who knows.' Jake sighed. 'Plan for the worst. Let's pretend this is your camp area. Can you tell me if there are any animals around, and where you should set up your tent?'

I turned 360° slowly in a clockwise direction, examining the landscape. Then I closed my eyes and stood, listening. I flared my nostrils, but all I could smell was Jake's cologne. I kept my eyes closed and pushed him downwind from me and started again, inhaling the breeze, listening.

'You have three minutes,' he snapped.

I ignored him. I squatted and dug my hands into the dirt, lifted it up and sniffed it deeply. Then I stood and pointed to a small hill. 'I'd go there first and see if there was a good, level spot with no mammoth tracks on it. Then –' I dodged a lightning fast kick, then blocked a punch. 'Cut it out. There *are* animals around. Over there is a dung heap, but it's dry and old. The dirt I dug up had a partial footprint in it. It looked feline. But there was no smell. Whatever was here, hasn't been around in a while. There's water over there,' I pointed to a copse of trees. 'Three birds swooped down into those trees since we've been here.'

'You're such a *wang ba* show-off,' Jake said. 'But you're right. There is water over there, there are felines around, and that hill might be a good site. But if you're wrong . . .' His voice trailed off.

'If I'm wrong, I'll probably get killed. I get that.'

Jake's mouth got tight, and I recognized the signs of hidden anger and stress. I wasn't sure why he was feeling either of those things, so I asked him.

'Don't you realize what you are about to do?' He breathed hard through his nose, then nodded towards the trees. 'Let's go. I don't know why I bother. Of course you realize on an intellectual level, but you have no idea, emotionally, what you are getting into. Anyone else would be nervous, terrified, even. You treat it like a . . . a trip to a zoo.'

I thought of what I'd overheard. Donnell Urbano had been speaking out of stress and nerves. I could understand that now. Jake implied I should be afraid. Actually, I was incapable of feeling fear. But I did know anxiety. I was anxious before a test, for example, or when I handed in a paper. Anxiety was linked to the unknown. I chased those thoughts away. Right now, we were looking for a campsite.

'Over there.' I pointed to a likely spot. 'There are no dead trees nearby that could fall in case of high winds. If it rains, the water will not flood my tent. I can set up a security perimeter.' I looked upwards. 'It is far enough away from that tree that nothing can climb it and jump onto my tent.'

'How do you know that?'

'The tree is over ten metres away!'

'A puma can easily leap ten metres.' Jake threw a punch at me, but I blocked it. 'So where will you set up your tent?' He feinted, then kicked. I blocked that too, but his next punch caught me on my sore shoulder.

'Stop hitting me, you fucking *sha bi*', I yelled.

Jake took a step back. 'Did I see an emotion there? Am I finally getting through to you?'

I thought about that. The news about a puma jumping ten metres had thrown me. 'You provoked me, but you were right.' I opened my floating screen and pointed to a diagram. 'Here is the security system I have – what do you suggest?'

'What can you tell me about it?'

I knew he was just testing me, but I went along. 'The system was

13

developed for use in areas with dangerous fauna. It consists of a force-field activated by a portable battery. You set up a perimeter with thin rods, then connect them with an electromagnetic field. You can adjust the strength depending on what is in the area,' I added.

'Get two sets,' he said. 'Make a double perimeter around your tent. If you have to camp under trees, clear away the branches and add an arc that will cross like this.' He drew two lines with his finger over the top of the drawing of my tent.

'If that falls, I'll get fried,' I said.

'Set it up so it can't fall. You're going to need something overhead if there are trees around. Think of the forcefield as making an igloo shape over your campsite. Don't think in two dimensions. Make sure your rods can be adjusted to do this.'

'Good idea. Will you look over the list of equipment the Time Senders are giving me and tell me if I need anything else?'

He opened the list and scrolled through it. His frown deepened as he read. 'What is this *ta ma de* stuff made of? It's all rapid bio-degrade products. What good is that if anything happens, and you outstay your week?'

'We can only take things that will disappear and not leave a trace in case anything happens to us. You know the rules.'

'Robin, *everything*, even a comlink, will disappear eventually. You're going so far back, you could leave your whole campsite there and no one from the modern world would know.'

I looked at Jake. 'What about our bodies? Modern medicine has left indelible traces on our teeth, bones – and I don't agree about our comlinks, or even ourselves, degrading. If we fall into a tar pit, if we get buried in a flash flood – our bodies, our technology, could be found. Traces of single-celled animals have been found as fossils, so don't you think our gear would show up too? There could be traces left over of our clothing, or even our food. We can't take any chances. Look, if it will make you feel better, we have special trans-mitters that we can set off if any emergency occurs. Help can be with us within hours. No scientist has ever been left behind – unlike the correctors.'

He shuddered. 'I know – what a *putain* job. Going back in time, knowing you'll never come back. But historians have been lost.'

'Only one. And one or two were recovered as dead bodies. I know. I'm not going to lie, it's not a trip to the zoo.' I waved my arm at the surrounding forest, 'But think, Jake. Scientists go back in pairs, we have a backup rescue team in case of need, and we have weapons, modern protection, unlike historians who have to go back and fit in. We rarely have to deal with humans.'

Jake looked up at the sky, then said, 'Tell me the truth. Is this about the typhus epidemic I've been hearing about?'

'I'm not supposed to talk about it.' I darted a glance at Jake's com-link and made a show of turning mine off. He got the hint and turned it off. 'Yes, it's about the typhus. Your dad must have told you something. He's been in touch with scientists in Siberia. They haven't found anything yet that will help, and I did some tests on the skeletons from the La Brea tar pits. Nothing conclusive.'

'My father said it was nearly eighty per cent fatal.'

'Oh, no. Actually, it's nearly a hundred per cent. It's some sort of mutant version and it infects animals and humans. There have only been a few cases in humans so far, but . . .' I broke off and grimaced. 'You know, the governments haven't been keeping this a secret, everyone has been remarkably open about this. The only thing that we're not saying is that we haven't been able to find a treatment or a vaccine. We're hoping that when we go back, we'll find the same disease, or something similar, killed off the big mammals and some of them will have antibodies.'

'I still don't want you to go.'

'That's too bad, because I'm going.'

Jake sighed. 'Right. You win. Anyhow, when has anything I've ever said or done changed your mind about anything?'

There was only one thing to do. I stepped in, grabbed his thigh between mine, slid my arms under his leg, and lifted – a classic *running the pipe move* that Jake could have avoided if he'd wanted. Instead, he pulled me after him, rolled over, and crushed me beneath him. The grass was thick enough here to soften our fall, and I didn't resist. On the contrary, I arched my back, grinding my pelvis into his.

This was not a new game for us. Since we'd known each other, we'd never ignored our mutual attraction. We ended up in bed together on a regular basis – sex with Jake was fantastic, and all he had to do was touch me and I felt a familiar tingle. I groaned in expectation, sliding my hands beneath his shirt, feeling his taut muscles and smooth skin. But this time, instead of kissing me, taking my clothes off, and ravishing me, he pushed me away.

'Stop, Robin.'

Surprised, I stopped moving. He was still lying on top of me and, according to my knowledge of human anatomy, he was aroused. I felt his hardness against my thigh. 'What is it? Are you mad at me? What did I do, and what can I do to help?' This happened often – people often lose their tempers with me, so I was careful to ask what the problem was so we could solve it together. Problem was, I was getting horny too, and that was clouding my thinking process. Usually I tried to keep my body well away from Jake. We had a chemistry that just wouldn't quit.

He rested his forehead on my shoulder. 'I already told you. I don't want to get emotionally involved with you. And when we . . . when . . . When we end up naked, tangled up together, it messes with my head.'

'You're being dramatic, Jake Powell. Cut out the, *"I don't want to fall in love with you"* bullshit and just fall in fucking love with me. Then we can have a normal relationship where you finally break up with Helen and call me every day, and I tell you you're my Prince Charming, and we end up married with one point two kids. Of course, then we'll probably divorce when I find out you've been having an affair with your secretary. *That's* normal. You telling me you don't want to fall in love with me, then making mad, passionate love to me, is *not* normal.'

'There is nothing normal about you, Robin.' He moaned then, and shivered, and I didn't have any problems getting his pants off, getting mine off, and guiding him into me.

Now, I should probably take the time to describe what happened in lurid detail, but let's just say we were both so turned on by that point that it was probably over before I could finish telling you about it. Afterwards, we got dressed, sat, shoulder to shoulder, and he told me that he would never have an affair with his secretary if we really did get married, and I told him that if he had any intention of marrying me he'd have to first break up with Helen.

He shook his head. 'Just concentrate on your trip to the past. We'll talk about this when you get back.'

'We've exhausted the subject,' I said, and oddly enough I felt a pang of sadness. Right now, I knew Jake was on an 'off' phase with the perfectly groomed, tenacious Helen, so I didn't have any qualms about jumping on him. When he was with her, I stayed away – she and I didn't appreciate each other. I thought her obsession with clothes and make-up was puerile, and she thought I was a sociopath. We were both right.

Chapter Three

After I was chosen to go back in time, the powers that be decided I needed to be re-evaluated. That didn't surprise me – I'd have been more surprised if I *hadn't* been subjected to a battery of tests. After all, I'd spent most of my adolescence in a juvenile facility for the mentally ill. But I'd survived and had been pronounced cured. Compared to prison, I suppose it was better. Compared to a boarding school, it was worse. There were ten or twenty of us at any given moment, and just like in a school, the ones that made it to the end of the treatment and 'graduated' were held up as shining examples. The treatment was brutal. The reward was freedom.

When I first got there, I was ten years old. I must have been the youngest patient, and I had no idea why I was there. I couldn't remember anything. I didn't even remember my name. At first I was isolated, but as it became obvious I was suffering from a real dissociative disorder and wasn't faking it, I got good care. They gave me psychotherapy counselling, psychosocial therapy, hypnosis, cognitive therapy, and antidepressants, anti-anxiety medications, and tranquillizers. But there were also shock treatments, sleep deprivation, cold showers, and the constant discomfort of twenty-four-hour lighting, narrow, uncomfortable beds, scratchy sheets, cold rooms and not enough warm blankets, poor food, and the grinding ugliness of the place. Some inmates chose the permanent way out.

The doctors used to say to us, '*In the end one needs more courage to live than to kill oneself.*' Some ancient French writer named Albert Camus said that. It's one of the stupid clichés the doctors were fond of telling us. They also used to say, '*What doesn't kill you, makes you stronger.*'

At night, fingers tracing faint cracks on the slick, green walls next to my bed, the twenty-four-hour lights making everything look bleached, I'd whisper, 'What doesn't kill me better run away fast.'

I'd be shivering with cold. Sometimes I'd be doubled up in pain, the drugs that they gave me making me sick. My head ached so badly sometimes I thought my skull would shatter. The worst wasn't the sleep deprivation; I hardly slept anyhow. The worst was the sadistic guard someone made the mistake of hiring. He never touched me, but he'd tap on my door at night. Softly, but loud enough for me to hear, he'd say, 'Tick, tick, tick, little girl.'

I complained, he denied it, and I got extra drugs to help me sleep. I was too scared to sleep though. He had the keys to my room. He never came in, and I would end up falling asleep exhausted by terror. In the hallways, if I walked by him, he'd say, 'Tick, tick, tick,' under his breath. The other inmates looked blank when I asked about him. I seemed to be the only person he tortured. For nearly all the years I was there, he was there too, but gradually he stopped paying attention to me, and one day he was gone. I suppose he'd been fired, or promoted to some other asylum. I never heard of him bothering anyone else, and that only made his treatment of me more unnerving.

I learned to sleep at night after he left. I learned what attitude to adopt in different situations, how to show emotion, even if I didn't really feel it. Sadness, joy, anger, boredom – these were all acquired traits. I learned to arrange my face, change my tone of voice, and one day, the director called me into his office and told me I was cured, and that my test scores had landed me in a prestigious university at only seventeen years of age.

I'd made a few friends in the asylum, but I'd always known that I'd be leaving, so I hadn't gotten close to anyone. I was pretty sure I'd never fit in anywhere. I was prepared to be alone, so it surprised me when I went to the university and had the best time of my life.

Sleeping in a comfortable bed with warm blankets helped. So did my roommate, a chatty, cheeky, bright girl named Yasmine. She invited me everywhere, even dragging me home with her on holidays, which was sheer bliss. I was surrounded by a boisterous, friendly family who thought I was great fun. Even when I told Yasmine about my childhood, it didn't change her attitude towards me. I had a best friend for life.

Her mother, Sing, became like a second mother, always welcoming, asking me how I was, and baking me my favourite dishes. Yasmine's brothers, twins younger than us by ten years, let me play their high-tech holo games with them. They taught me how to go virtual surfing, skydiving, and oceanic exploring – all the games I'd missed growing up in a psychiatric ward. Her father was a philosopher and sage – I was in awe of him, but he encouraged me when I failed my tests, kept my spirits up, and kept me going when all I wanted to do was quit. I still have a poem that he wrote for me. I never thought that someone would write a poem just for me. It was an amazing gift. In fact, Yasmine's whole family was like a gift to me. I cherished them.

I kept each of those years in my memory, encapsulated in gold. Shiny and precious. After three years, we graduated and I applied to Tempus University to continue my Masters degree in environmental threats, which was also when I started working for Dr Powell. Yasmine went to law school and became a lawyer. We managed to see each other nearly every week. She was my anchor. She was also my advisor.

'Yasmine, are you busy?' I opened a floating screen and hit play.

'Hey, girl. Just busy dying, that's all.' It was Yasmine. She lay on her hospital bed, wires and tubes sticking out of her everywhere.

We'd made the films when she knew it was finished. She'd fought so hard. But I could never bear to let her go.

'I'm fine with it,' she said, 'but don't show my mother until she asks to see them. Promise.'

I asked her questions, made her talk, she had ideas too. Sometimes she gave me specific dates to do things. 'Don't open this vid until your thirtieth birthday,' she said, sending me a file. I haven't looked yet.

'Yasmine, I'm going back in time. I'm going to see sabre-toothed tigers, and maybe a mammoth or two. What do you say to that?'

'Whatever you do, it will be wonderful,' she said, a little breathless. Her pupils were huge with drugs but her gaze was clear.

'I had an evaluation today and I passed. After the asylum, the brain-crackers at the University are like kittens. But they asked some good questions. The thing that bothers everyone is my amnesia, but you were right. Every year that goes by makes it more plausible and less problematic. Even to me it seems like something that happened to someone else. I'm starting to feel *normal*, Yaz.'

'Tell me more. I'm listening.'

'Well, the evaluation lasted for ages, but at least Donnell will get the results and hopefully he'll stop trying to get me kicked off the team. The dean is on my side, and so is Dr Powell.'

'I'm so proud of you, Robin. You'll be fantastic.'

'I know you're just saying that.' I put my hand out and touched the screen, where her arm lay on the bed. My hand made ripples in the vid.

'You're making me all wobbly,' she said, and laughed.

I loved this tape. She was still able to laugh. Oh, damn, how I missed her. 'I miss you,' I said. It wasn't in the script, but I said it anyhow.

She reached out and patted where my hand would be. 'Wherever you go, whatever you do, if you think of me, I'll be with you.' Her smile was radiant.

I let the vid run, just wanting to hear her voice. I missed her, she was a hole in my chest. I'd never get over it. Before the vid ran out, she looked straight at me and said, 'If you ever get into trouble, if you ever need anything, if you're ever in dire need. Just call me. Do you hear that? Call me.'

Strangely comforted, I turned the tape off and went to take a shower.

Chapter Four

The first test took place in a controlled environment. We had to set up a campsite, then deal with whatever the people administering the test threw at us. We met at the training centre, a huge building that belonged to the army corps but was shared with Tempus U. We'd arrived in the morning, been subjected to a bunch of physicals, blood taken, peed in a jar, had dinner in the cafeteria, then went to our dormitory. At about five a.m., by my reckoning, they woke us up and told us to get our gear and meet in the hallway. *Our gear?* First part of the test was sifting through a mountain of camping shit and choosing a backpack, tent, and supplies. They didn't tell us how long the test would last. If you didn't take enough you'd fail – if you took too much you'd probably fail too, but not as badly.

I tried to talk to Donnell, explain that I thought it might be a good idea to split up some of the supplies, but he snapped at me, told me to just pack and shut the fuck up.

Fine. I could deal with that. Easier and less energy than explaining, but it wasn't intelligent planning. So instead, I commented aloud on everything I took and why, hoping he'd pitch in. I had a list and called it up on a floating screen via my comlink. The list was succinct:

Navigation. Sun protection. Insulation. Clothing. Illumination. First-aid kit. Repair kit and tools. Nutrition.

I looked at the imposing pile of gear, then took a deep breath and started. 'Backpack, sixty-five hundred cubic cm, with alu-frame. Sleeping bag. Tent. Storm sheet. Mylar bags for storing food. Fourteen high-protein food packs. Water pouches. Hygiene kit for body and teeth. Two packs of super-thin energy poles for perimeter twenty meters diameter. A medbot. I'm going to wear warm hiking clothes, and I'm taking these boots. Oh, look, fishing gear!' This was spur of the moment, but it had caught my eye. So had a small fire-starting kit. Both fishing and fire kit looked ridiculously antique, but both fit in my pocket. I kept up my monologue. 'I need stuff for my samples and a recording device. Both have to be lightweight and waterproof. I'll take a scribe, and I'll take an extra solar battery pack for the perimeter fence and for the recording devices. Binoculars. Night vision goggles with audio intensifiers. Microscope. Chemical water purifier and a small portable lab to run some basic tests. What do you have, Donnell?'

He paused, then said, 'Same as you, except I took weapons, an axe, and a shovel. Since I'll be doing the filming, I have all the camera, holo, and vid equipment. Can you take extra food for me as I'll be carrying more weight than you will? I'll delegate meals to you.'

'Fine.' I took no offence at his suggestion. In fact, I was glad that he'd started communicating with me. Doing meals would be mostly opening the slop packs, as they were called, and then disposing of any waste so that animals wouldn't be attracted to the smell. I'd taken a small shovel as well, and an axe sounded like a good idea. I found one that had a flat/hammer side. And in the first-aid kit, I made sure there was a strong painkiller and anti-diarrhoea medicine, along with tampons and isopropyl alcohol.

A buzzer rang and suddenly voices rang out. 'Grab your gear! Over here! Right now!'

I slung my backpack on, wincing at its weight, and gave a voice command to my float-vid. It folded up and beamed itself into my comlink. I patted my chest pocket to make sure I had my vitapak then I shuffled after Donnell, hoping I'd not forgotten anything. At the doorway armed guards met us and escorted us at a quick trot down an endless hallway. They took us to a small room and shut the door on us.

'What happens—'

'Just wait and see,' said Donnell. He'd done this before, but he still looked apprehensive.

Then a robotic voice intoned: *'Tractor beam in three, two, one.'*

A pale blue light appeared out of the ceiling and shone on us. I suppose this was what the tractor beam looked like. I'd never seen the real one. Then a door in front of us opened and the floor tilted, sending us skidding and sliding into pitch darkness and pouring rain.

I flicked my wrist and a rain-breaker shot out of my sleeve and covered me. I must have looked like a lumpy, shiny black pyramid – if you could see anything. I fumbled in my pocket and put on a pair of night-vision goggles. Just then Donnell turned on a flashlight and just about fried my eyeballs. 'Ow, *merde!* Turn that *ta ma de* thing away from me!'

'Just making sure you were all right.' He shone the beam away from me, and I stood squinting as black dots chased themselves across my vision.

With my goggles, and his flashlight, I could see we were standing in a fast-running stream at the bottom of a ravine. A jumble of rocks and boulders, some shoulder-height, rose on either side of us. 'Left or right?' I asked. 'Both sides look about the same. On the right, I can see the tops of some trees. On the left, it looks empty, like a grassland. Hard to see without climbing up and checking.'

'Let's go to the left then. I don't want to do trees in the dark. Who knows what's in them.' Donnell put the flashlight on his head, it doubled as a headlamp, and started to climb.

'Right.' He might be able to climb with a fifty-pound weight on his back, but I could not. I unslung my backpack and hefted it up onto the nearest boulder, then climbed after it.

'Don't lose that,' he said sternly, pointing at my pack.

'It's tied to my harness. You can't see it. It's under my rain-breaker.' I was glad of the rain-breaker. It was light and espoused my arms and legs, keeping me dry. It had a hood with a visor, and it could double as a raft, because it was inflatable. It was also camouflage, turning dark or light to blend with the background. It was mine, actually. I didn't dig it out of the pile of gear. It looked like a simple bracelet, but if you flipped your wrist a certain way, it became the rain-breaker. It had cost me a month's salary, but I loved gadgets like these.

My foot slipped and I turned my attention back to the climb. Suddenly I heard a low rumble coming from upstream. *'Wo cao!'* shouted Donnell. 'Flash flood. Move it!'

I moved it.

We barely made it to the top of the last boulder when the rumble became a roar, and white water churned into the ravine, reaching nearly halfway up the sides. We were stuck on this side for now. Hopefully we'd made a good choice. We wouldn't be heading for the trees any time soon.

As I crawled over the lip of the ravine, I looked around. The night-vision goggles showed me rain slashing onto a prairie. I couldn't see very far into the gloom. Even Donnell's headlamp, although on high beam, barely lit up the scene. I put my hand on the ground, trying to see if the rain was running in any certain direction. The ground was sodden, the water was soaking into it.

'We should move away from the edge of the ravine,' I shouted over the crashing river and the pouring rain.

'Agreed. Where to?'

'Upstream,' I said, pointing. 'Let's try for higher ground.'

'You go first.' He took a rifle from his pack and armed it. He put on night-vision goggles and turned his headlamp off. 'No use advertising our presence any more than we have to,' he said grimly. Then he put his audio amplifiers in his ears and turned them up. With hand motions, he told me to be silent. The sound of the rain must have been deafening. I wondered if he could hear anything over that. I put mine on, and I realized they tuned out ambient sounds such as wind and rain. In an instant, there was silence except for the sound of our breathing and footsteps.

We left the banks of the ravine; the ground was too unstable, and we slogged through waist-high grass. We headed uphill; I could feel the slope although I could not see it. After a short time – maybe a quarter of an hour – the grass gave way to scrub brush and instead of mud, there were rocks underfoot. I stopped and motioned to

Donnell. We were on the crest of a hill, and in the daylight, could probably see a good distance around us. I mimed setting up a tent, and he nodded. I put my backpack down and pulled out my perimeter fence, setting the rods in a double circle as Jake had suggested. Before activating it, I took a stick and poked it along the ground where I wanted to set up the tents. I was careful to look for burrows and to check under rocks. In the rain, snakes and poisonous insects could be hiding, only to come out under the shelter of the tents.

I didn't find anything, so I activated the perimeter. Only then did I relax. Donnell had already set up his tent and had crawled inside. I noted that he'd taken the only flat spot available. Fine, I could make do. I got my shovel out and scraped and dug a relatively smooth spot. When my tent was up, I checked the time. It was nearly six a.m. The sun would be rising soon. The rain still hadn't let up, so I wasn't sure how soon the light would get to us. There wasn't the faintest smudge of grey on the horizon. I took off my boots, set my alarm, and lay down in my tent, clothes and all, intent on getting at least a half hour's rest. I didn't waste time lying awake and worrying. The safety perimeter was up, I still had my amplifiers in my ears, so I'd hear if anything came in contact with it. I fell asleep nearly at once.

My alarm woke me out of a sound sleep. Donnell was still in his tent, so I called up a vidcam and scanned the area around us, putting the info into a floating vid-map. There was no sign of life. The rain had tapered off, but low clouds obscured the sky. The vidcam had an infrared lens but nothing showed up. I deactivated the perimeter fence and went downhill about a hundred metres to dig a latrine pit. Then I went to the edge of the ravine and carefully peered over. The flash flood had diminished, but the water was still too deep and wild to attempt a safe crossing. With a long rope, I lowered my canteen into it and filled it with water, then pulled it up and fastened it to my belt. I never had my back turned to the land around me. I kept the vidcam turned on and the floating screen in front of me. That's how I saw Donnell step out of the camp and head towards me.

'Latrine?' he called.

'Downhill a-ways. You'll see. I left my shovel next to it.' I coiled the rope and put it in my pocket.

'Right. Can you send your floating screen over? I'm having problems with mine. Also, I want you to get a reading from that water; see what lifeforms are in it.' He strode off downhill without waiting for an answer, so I sent my screen over to him and jogged to the campsite to get more sample jars. Once there, I spotted something shiny over by the edge of the ravine. Odd. What was my axe doing there? I could have sworn it was in my tent. I must have dropped it last night in the rain, in the dark, as I set up the perimeter. Not good. I put my canteen down in front of my tent and went over to the ravine. I bent to pick up my axe. I didn't think the ground could give away so fast. One minute I was on solid ground, the next I was in free-fall. I flailed, but there was nothing to grab hold of, no roots, branches, or tufts of grass.

I hit water, which was better than landing on rocks, but the flood swept me downstream and I crashed against several boulders before I managed to latch on to one. Water surged over my head but I held on and got one foot braced on a rock just behind me. Pushing against the current, I lifted my face out of the water and took a gasping breath. I didn't try to crawl out of the water just yet. First I had to get a better grip on the boulder. When I thought I was secure, I shoved with my foot and hoisted myself onto the rock. The current grabbed my legs and tried to drag me back but I kicked and pulled, and managed to get out of the river's grip. I swore. The force of the water had stripped one of my boots off and my left wrist felt sprained. I sent a message to Donnell and stood up on my boulder, looking for a way up the sides of the ravine.

'Stay away from the edge,' I yelled, when I saw him. 'Wait, take my rope. Help me climb up the side.' I tied one end around my waist then tossed the other end up to him.

Prudently, he withdrew, and a moment later, said, 'The rope is secure. Go ahead!'

One-handed, I climbed up the ravine. Donnell had staked the rope and held it steady for me. I topped the edge of the ravine then slithered on my stomach until I was sure I wasn't going to start another landslide. Then I stood up, shook water out of my hair, and looked around. I'd gone downstream quite a-ways. Donnell had the floating screen on, and he was keeping an eye on it.

'If you're finished with your bath, we have a lot to do,' he said.

I was glad he wasn't going to berate me about falling into the river, so I just nodded and sloshed up the hill. Luckily, I had another pair of boots in my pack.

We worked together all day, setting up blinds, cameras with motion sensors, and sending our vidcams out to scan the area. We hiked away from the campsite to eat, and I made sure we put everything that smelled even vaguely like food into Mylar bags and sealed them. The day passed quickly. There were no signs of life, but this was just a test, so I wasn't expecting anything.

At two in the morning, loud screeches woke me. Something had hit the perimeter fence. I yelled 'Fiat lux!' and spotlights flooded the area.

Three baboons circled the campsite, chattering and leaping from rock to rock. When they saw us, they ran away, disappearing into the night.

Donnell looked at me and laughed. 'Fiat lux?'

'"Let there be light" works too. Or just yell "lights",' I said. But I was frowning. 'Actually, I'd set it up so that any loud noise would trigger the light. The apes' screeching should have done that.' I looked at my comlink and said, 'Verify audio settings on perimeter fence.'

We sent a vidcam to follow the apes as they left the area. We discovered that the infrared lens worked better than the night-vision lens. The rest of the short night we spent testing the security measures we were planning on taking on our trip. I said I'd rather have a larger perimeter, to give more warning, but Donnell said it would be hard to transport and maintain for just one week. We agreed that there had to be an audio as well as a visual signal, and that we'd set up cams at night. When the sun came up, we'd left the campsite and were sitting around a small fire, drinking coffee, talking about our miserable childhoods – trying to outdo each other with sad stories.

'Did you really grow up in an asylum?' he asked me.

'Yes. I had a traumatic experience that erased my memory. I can't recall anything before the age of ten. Does that make you uncomfortable?'

He laughed. 'I can barely remember anything that happened last year, much less when I was ten.' He paused. 'You know, I was born in the Still United States of the South. My parents left and took me across the border clandestinely into the Western State of California when I was seven.'

I didn't know that. 'Did you hear anything about the "Event", as they call it, that split the once United States into three parts?' I was curious. I'd missed out on my childhood because everything was a blank until I was age ten, and then I'd been interned in the psychiatric ward. But growing up in the Still United States of the South – *that* must have been hard. From my history lessons, I knew that the poor had been enslaved by the wealthy, and a huge purge had wiped out anyone who wasn't a strict Evangelical, or anyone who didn't conform – or wouldn't conform.

Donnell shook his head. 'I don't remember too much about the South. I know some of my family tried to make it to the Kingdom of Brazil – but they never made it. Brazil wouldn't let any of the "unwashed poor" over their border. My family was poor. Luckily, they were extremely devout and their skin was the right colour. As pale as milk. They let us live in compounds full of other workers. They called us the blessed ones, but we didn't feel blessed. My parents recognized early on that we were just serfs. They started planning their escape nearly right after the "Event".' He gave a dry laugh. '*Event.* Stupid name for a total collapse of the government because of starvation brought on by agricultural failure.'

'Were your people farmers?'

'We had a cotton and peanut farm. One of my first memories is playing in the red dirt, when there was enough water for mixing clay. Then came the drought, the famine, and my family chose to go south instead of north.'

'They probably thought they were doing the right thing,' I said. At that time, in the North, there were food riots while the East and the

West were splitting, Canada had sided with California, there were no safe choices. 'Your parents couldn't have known that the South would close the borders so fast, that the North would recover because of the Green Deal, and that the Kingdom of Brazil would use its army.'

'My parents were proud Southerners, religious bigots, who thought they were escaping the Sodom and Gomorrah of the North. They soon changed their minds when my three older sisters were taken to be brides of the Community.' He sighed. 'I never saw them again. I don't know if they are still alive. My parents managed to get me out. For that, I'll always be grateful.'

'Where are they now? They must be proud of you,' I asked.

'They died when I was in college. They'd always been in poor health. My father went first, my mother followed soon after. I don't have any family left in The Western State of California, but I do have cousins on Mars and I visit them every year. Here, look at the holos I have.'

I admired the projections. He told me he'd probably retire there. I thought it looked claustrophobic, living in huge cities underground or under huge domes, but he loved the technology, and I had to admit, the holos were amazing.

'It's so civilized there, you have no idea. No problems left over from the Event, no dead zones, no main religion to kowtow to, and everyone is prosperous. The mines on Mars, and the satellite and asteroid mines, all contribute to a strong economy.' Donnell nodded and sipped his coffee. 'The only thing I'd miss are blue skies, but inside the domes they can even make that happen.'

'That sounds *wo cao*', I said, and didn't care if he thought I meant awesome when I really meant fucking awful. I shivered. I would hate to live on Mars, but thousands, no, millions of people had already paid to take the next settler ship to that planet. It was scheduled for lift-off sometime this year – as soon as it got clearance from Mars Corp, the corporation/government that ran the planet. But there were problems. Rumours had started that the settlers were sick. And that was another thing that made our trip so urgent. A vaccine had to be found before the Mars Corp shut the space ports on Mars. If that happened, millions of people on Earth would die. Both from typhus, and from what they were really fleeing – a famine had struck the Still United States of the South. Millions had been coming with horror stories about what was happening. The Kingdom of Brazil had shut its borders to refugees again. Right now they were in a sort of giant encampment near the southern border; a teeming mass of hope, dreams, and despair. And if the typhus ever reached them . . . it didn't bear thinking about. Our voyage back in time was their last chance. If we didn't get enough samples to make a vaccine, the Mars Corp would never let them in, and the Western State of California was already at full capacity. If the typhus hit them, the Western State of California would have no choice but to quarantine them. A million men, women, and children. The new strain of typhus was nearly one hundred per cent fatal. You do the maths.

The test ended soon after that. We didn't have any more baboons but a tiger, obviously more used to pacing in a zoo cage than wandering around free, blundered into our encampment one evening, setting off the alarms again. The shock upset the tiger so much he just sat and cried as we reset the alarm. When the alarm stopped, he lay down and licked his sore paws. I supposed he'd been starved then set loose near our camp. I sighed, took one of my instant meals, opened it, and threw it to the tiger. He gulped it down and looked at me hopefully. I gazed up at the sky (they had to be observing us) and yelled, 'That's fucking pathetic – I don't think there are zoo animals in the Palaeolithic. Can't you think of something else?'

Soon after, a group of armed men in army fatigues marched up and ordered us to follow them. We broke camp and hiked to the pickup point, which we were supposed to memorize, but that I'd completely forgotten to memorize (if I'd had to grab the real beam back in time, I would have missed the bus), but I pretended to know exactly where it was. We stepped into the blue light. Then a helicopter came and picked us up.

31

Chapter Five

The next two weeks were spent doing more tests, although we didn't have any more camping trips. An animal behavioural expert came and bored us to death with a never-ending lesson. I think he just loved the sound of his own voice, because he repeated each phrase two or three times. We learned that lions were social animals but that tigers were not, and that wolves lived in packs and had a strict social hierarchy. I raised my hand.

'Like chickens and humans?' I asked.

His glare told me I'd probably overestimated his sense of humour.

'Sorry. What about sabre-toothed tigers? What can you tell me about them? And can you be concise? I don't have much more memory on my vidcam's disc,' I asked, meaning to placate. I think that if I hadn't yawned in the middle of the question, his answer would have been different. As it was, his reply was unhelpful, unless I was thinking of harming myself with my vidcam.

We went over our respective missions. Donnell was to film everything, get good footage for the museum, and protect me. I was supposed to get samples from the animals – Donnell had permission to tranquillize if possible and if security measures could be met, otherwise I would scout out carrion. I needed blood, fur, fleas, ticks, saliva, bones – just about anything I could get. We needed to compare the pathogens from the past to the one ravaging our world, and see if a vaccine could be made. Although people at the Centre didn't tell me a hundred times a day, I felt their anxiety. I had to get those samples and I needed to hurry. Some had family wanting to go to Mars. Some had friends. Some had applied for themselves, and would soon be transferred to the ever-growing immigration holding area. Mars was treating everyone, even the scientists at our lab, like refugees.

As for myself and my mission, I kept waiting to get notice that I'd been replaced, but either Donnell had decided to keep me, or the dean had refused to change his mind, because no one came to remove me from the training centre. I applied myself to putting together the best collecting kit I could.

The night before we left, we went to the infirmary for the final touch. Everything we had with us, every piece of clothing and technology, was made to degrade within weeks. Everything was treated with a substance that would basically melt it into sludge. And the scariest part of all was getting the capsule containing that same substance injected into our bodies.

Dr Grace Feldman was reassuring. 'Now, don't worry. These cannot release until fully ten days have passed. We used to set them for eight, but it was proving stressful for the travellers. Now we have ten-day capsules. All you have to do is make sure you come see us when you get back. Don't forget, now!'

'Is that a joke? Have any time travellers forgotten?' I asked.

Donnell rolled his eyes, and the doctor turned to her assistant, who was carrying a small metal tray. 'Put them down there.'

The assistant placed the tray on the edge of the table and it tipped. Both capsules flew into the air. Reflexively, I reached out and grabbed them. I looked at them. Small, about the size of a wasp, and with the same yellow and black stripes. I looked closer. 'Cool, our names are on them. Look, Donnell, this one is yours!'

He scowled. 'Put those down, *bèn dàn*. Now we have to sterilize them again.'

'Oh, sorry!' I looked at Dr Feldman. 'I wasn't thinking. I didn't want them to hit the floor. If it broke, would it melt the floor?' I tossed the little capsules into the tray, one into the section with my name on it, the other into Donnell's section. 'I just can't imagine anyone forgetting to remove it. Has anyone melted? Can you tell me what happens—'

'Robin, that's enough,' snarled Donnell, and the doctor looked at him in surprise. She'd been chuckling at my banter.

'They are unbreakable, and the injector sterilizes them,' she replied, slipping a capsule into the injector. She pressed it against my thigh and shot the capsule into my leg. It only stung for a few seconds.

She injected Donnell's capsule, then made us thumbprint an electronic contract saying that we agreed to show up there before the ten days' expiration date was past in order to have the capsules removed, and that if for some reason we couldn't make it back, we wouldn't hold them responsible.

'I feel like a time bomb,' I said to Donnell.

He winced. 'Get some sleep. We have a long day tomorrow.'

Finally it was *The Day*. I was actually going back in time. I hadn't been able to see Jake, or Dr Powell, or anyone except the doctors, the professors, the wildlife expert, and Donnell. I have to admit that I was starting to appreciate him. He had an enormous responsibility as expedition leader, but he had a sort of deep calm about him. He never raised his voice, never complained, and although I doubted he had the slightest wish to take me with him, he never let on that he'd tried to get me kicked off his team.

We woke up before dawn and made our way to the sending room. I'd never been there. It was vast, with a glass dome overhead. Before sufficient energy could be stored, the Time Senders had to use lightning. Nowadays the energy is collected continuously and kept beneath the building in a huge, cone-shaped force field. There is probably enough energy stored there to shoot the entire University into space. Hopefully that would never happen. But I always imagine a sort of mega-volcano with all its energy and pressure held back by a giant clamp holding it shut. The volcano swells, the pressure builds, and then the clamp is released, and the explosion is channelled into a vacuum. And that happens over and over, each time someone voyages back in time. The secret is making particles go faster than the speed of light and of course the particles I'm talking about are our atoms. We're basically frozen, then unravelled atom by atom, and projected into a vacuum where our atoms are shot into a sort of hadron collider. The programming is done using quartz, and starlight as the clock, and believe me, even if I had the slightest idea how it was done, I probably couldn't explain it to a layman. And I don't know how it's done. Well, I know there is something about light coming from stars; the scientists use light that's travelled a certain amount of time. And I know that our atoms are immutable so they can be taken apart but they will always snap together in exactly the same order they started out as. That way, we don't leave as human beings and arrive as pineapples, for example.

What they don't tell you is how incredibly painful it is.

I think I started screaming at '*seven, six, five . . .*' and had passed out by the time '*four*' came along.

'Oh, my head, Oh, *fuck, fuck*, fuck,' I moaned between clenched teeth.

'*Wo cao*,' gasped Donnell. 'It never gets any easier.' He coughed. '*Wo cao*. What a trip.' He rolled over and retched.

I lay with my face in the grass. I hadn't vomited, but that's only because I couldn't take a full breath. I knew that as soon as my diaphragm started working again I'd spill my guts. It didn't take long. 'Why, oh why, did I agree to this,' I said, between bouts of retching and paralysing pain. Finally, I managed to get to my knees. 'What if a sabre-toothed tiger had been here? We'd already be eaten, or worse.'

He shook his head. 'See how the air around us is faintly blue? We're protected by the tractor beam for a good hour. Nothing can get in.'

I reached out my hand and touched the blue-tinged air. It was a little like being surrounded by a very faint fog. I poked. My finger tingled and stung. '*Wo cao!*' I said. As I watched, the blue shivered and began to fade. 'It's almost gone. Let's go. We should send some vidcams out and see if there are any spots that look like a good campsite.'

Donnell looked at his comlink.

'What time is it?' I asked. 'Is time here different, I wonder? It was nearly noon when we left the, um, future.' I glanced at my own

35

comlink. 'It's one minute to one. Amazing. We go back twelve thousand years in little more than an hour. A-*fucking*-mazing. Look at this place!' Mouth open in amazement, I gazed around. We were on the side of a grassy hill, and we had a good view of the surrounding area. I forgot about my pain, I was in the past! I was here! I staggered to my feet and looked around. '*Wa cao!* We're really here! There is a *ta me da* giant armadillo down there. *Putain,* a glyptodon! This is amazing. Look at that! It looks like a walking igloo except it's brown, not white. Donnell, *look!*'

Donnell didn't look at the scenery. He looked at me, and said, 'Robin, I just wanted to say I'm sorry. I'm really very sorry. I didn't have a choice in the matter.' He looked truly upset.

I hastened to reassure him. 'No need to apologize. Look, I know you didn't want to have me as a partner. I overheard you talking to the dean. It doesn't matter. Let's just make this trip a success. We have many lives depending on us.'

He made a strange noise. Then his face turned ashen, and he gagged like he was about to be sick. I thought he was still feeling the effects of the trip. I bent to help him to his feet, but he gagged again, then screamed.

'What is it? Donnell? What is happening?' I didn't understand what I was seeing. His leg, *his leg was shrinking.* He shrieked, grabbed his leg, and his hands sank into his, well, where his thigh should have been, and then he sort of slid and slumped to the ground, convulsing, his body moving as if waves were tossing it, as if he were made of liquid, and his clothes became wet, and the strongest, strangest smell assaulted my nose.

I think I started to scream then too. Then my breath ran out and all I could do was squeak, squeak, squeak, as I tried to drag air into my lungs.

He must have been in dreadful pain. He screamed until the end. Until all that was left was his chest and his head, then those too sank into themselves and all that was left were clothes and boots, and a pink, foamy gel.

I spun around and flailed at the air, at the faint wisp of blue that still lingered. I found my voice. 'Help!' I screamed, 'Help, help, help!'

No one came. Below me, in the valley, the glyptodon lifted its head and seemed to look in my direction.

I couldn't stop shaking, and I couldn't seem to be able to breathe. Black spots danced in front of my vision and I knelt down, bent over, and hit my head on the ground. 'No. No. No! That didn't just happen. It's a hallucination. You're still unconscious. You'll wake up in a minute. Wake up, Robin. Wake the feck up.' I dug my fingers into the dirt and screamed again.

The smell was still horrible. I got up and, not looking at the strange pile of slime that had been Donnell, I moved away. I'd staggered halfway down the hill when I realized I didn't know where my gear was. Had it appeared with us? I hadn't even checked. I had to go back. I stood still, my fists clenched. 'I can do this,' I said.

I went back uphill and saw our gear scattered about ten metres away from – from the accident. It had to have been an accident. But how? The doctor said that the capsules were unbreakable and set for ten days. *Shit shit shit!* I still had a capsule in my leg. *No. Oh, no, I couldn't melt.* I panicked. I do my best work when I panic. It's amazing what I can do when I think I'm about to turn into a pile of pink mucus.

I ripped open my vest pocket, grabbed my vitapak, and tore off my pants. 'Scalpel,' I gasped. 'Scalpel and antiseptic. *Putain*, that hurts! *Putain-putain-putain!*' I dug and swore until I found the little yellow wasp-like capsule. I threw it as far as I could into the grass. 'Cauterize,' I ordered, pressing the edges of the wound together and crying with pain as the vitapak seared the cut closed. *'Argh!* Anaesthesia! I'm such a fecking *bèn dàn sha bi*! Anaesthesia! *Please!'* My vitapak injected a dose of painkiller and numbed my leg. If only I'd thought of that before I'd hacked at myself.

I trembled, holding my vitapak with bloody hands, as my tears plopped on my naked leg. I shook with pain and shock, but at the same time, I was submerged with relief. I wasn't going to melt.

I was just going to get eaten.

Down in the valley, a pack of huge dire wolves appeared. As I watched, they surged out from under the trees and surrounded the glyptodon, but the glyptodon, towering over them and encased in an impenetrable armour, ignored them and continued grazing. I knew that the dire wolves would pick up my scent any minute now, so I pulled my pants over my bloody leg and grabbed the pack with my security perimeter rods. Looking quickly around, I saw that I was on a hill, but behind me the land rose steeply and I couldn't see what was over the rise. In front of me, the grassy valley stretched left and right following the curve of a wide river, while past that was a thick forest. I didn't like not knowing what was behind me, so I called up my floating screen and sent a cam. The hill was steep, there were small bushes, then it levelled off and became a large bluff overlooking a river. The bluff was high, maybe forty or fifty metres, and the view was spectacular. From there, I could see the scrub oak forest and the winding, grassy valley on this side of the river. And on the other side of the river, a forest of giant spruce trees stretched for as far as I could see. Sedge grass grew in huge clumps in the marshland around the river, and several smaller streams glinted in the distance.

I decided to head for the bluff. There were boulders scattered here and there, and I could use them for cover if needed. Keeping an eye on the wolf pack, I started hiking up the hillside. If the dire wolves started after me I'd have time to set up a quick safety perimeter, but I could only take one backpack at a time. Mine held most of the food but I wasn't worried about eating, I wanted protection. Donnell's held the weapons, so I grabbed his, swore at its weight, and started walking.

It didn't take long to get to the top of the bluff. I quickly set up a perimeter then I looked down the hill at my backpack and decided to risk getting it. The dire wolves were concentrating on the glyptodon. I had thought they would ignore it, but they were running at it, one at a time, from different angles, and the hulking glyptodon was getting annoyed. It tucked its head into its massive shell and swung its heavy tail, keeping the wolves at bay.

I jogged back down the hill and had almost reached my backpack when a sort of tingle ran up my spine, and I saw a movement in the grass not far from me. Two of the wolves had snuck up on me. I'd been distracted by the other wolves' attack on the glyptodon. But these two hadn't cared about the giant armadillo. They had scented my blood, and were stalking me.

I froze, then turned and pelted back up the hill. The dire wolves hurled themselves after me. I leapt through the stubby brush, topped the rise, threw myself on the ground and rolled into the perimeter, shouting, 'En garde!'

The perimeter sizzled as it activated and then there came a shower of sparks and yelps as the first dire wolf came into contact with the force field. Breathing in huge, gulping sobs, I scrambled to take shelter behind a boulder. The wolves snarled and whined. The one who'd been stung stayed back, but its mate jumped at one of the rods, snarling and yelping when it was shocked. I opened my floating screen and watched the dire wolves as they paced just outside the perimeter. They were very large, but looked thin. I estimated the bigger one at about 70 or 80 kilos, his back was easily as high as my sternum. The smaller one would have reached my waist, and probably weighed slightly more than I did – 60 kilos or so. Their fur was rough and looked matted in areas, and I saw open sores on their ears and legs.

I put my floating screen away and dug around in Donnell's backpack, looking for his hover-cams. As filmmaker, he was supposed to have all that gear, but I could only find one vidcam. I put his pack down and frowned. This was his pack, in it were his tent, his rifles, extra clothes, and boots. I found a sleeping bag and what looked like a portable lab. Could that be for processing the films? I shook my head. Maybe I was still in shock and wasn't seeing things right.

Another yelp and snarl sounded, and then more snarls. I turned, and saw the whole pack was now on the bluff. They had just been playing with the glyptodon. I'd been the real prey all along. The two largest dire wolves were sitting closest to the perimeter; Every now and then, one would approach just close enough to feel the static electricity in the air. The dire wolf would snap and snarl, then go sit down again. None of the wolves in the pack looked very healthy. Whatever was killing the mammals may possibly have infected them as well.

Some of the smilodon bones that I'd studied had tested positive for Typhus-77 but no one had tested the bones of any other species. We'd just assumed that it came from the smilodons. Typhus-77 had such similarities with feline typhus – nearly the same mortality rate, same symptoms, same pathology – that we hypothesize that the virus came from smilodon carcasses dating from the Ice Age, and that this ancient feline typhus had mutated to infect humans. Scientists had always thought that the extinction of the large mammals in North America came about due to humans, who had appeared on the scene just before the animals started to die out. Such a massive, quick extinction of so many different species didn't fit with the profile of a virus. Now, I watched the dire wolves and wondered if I hadn't been amiss by not testing other fossils.

Two of the wolves started fighting. It didn't last long, but it was a bloody fight. I marked the area in my memory. After they left, I'd collect some samples. Things were looking up. Except I was hungry and thirsty and had no food or drink.

I rubbed my face. I should have grabbed my backpack. At least I'd have food and water. Donnell hadn't brought anything. Which was stupid. Or maybe he had another pack and I hadn't seen it. I felt secure behind my perimeter, but I took more rods and set up another one, trying not to look at the huge dire wolves slavering just outside. Then I pitched Donnell's tent and searched through his things for something to start a fire with.

In his tool kit, he had a firestarter among other things. I nearly didn't examine the small black gadget that fell at my feet. But I picked it up and turned it over. It was marked 'In Case of Emergency'. I slumped in relief. The emergency was now. I could call and the rescue team would come. It would take a couple of days – but they would come. And I would be rescued. You were only supposed to use the call as a last resort in case of an emergency. If your partner suddenly melting into a puddle didn't qualify as an emergency, I didn't know what did. I kissed the box then opened it, flipped the switch, and fell over backwards when a blue light shot out of it with an unholy screech.

The wolves fled. The blue light, the noise, it was all too much. I followed them with the vidcam until they vanished in the forest, and then I ran out and collected samples. There were tufts of fur, some drops of blood, and even a small chunk of skin. I put it all away and then hiked down the hill to pick up my backpack.

I grabbed it, then ran back up the hill. Panting, I looked at the floating screen. No dire wolves. The glyptodon was heading off towards the river. I thought about things, and decided I couldn't just leave Donnell's remains, or rather, what remained of Donnell, on the slope like that. I could put some stones over it, that would be more respectful than letting the rain wash him away.

I piled some stones on the slime. Even his clothes had started to dissolve. Then I looked to see if he hadn't brought another pack with his film equipment. There was nothing. But something caught my eye. I went closer, then froze. It was the capsule I'd dug out of *my* leg. I nearly took off running, but it was glinting in the grass and I was afraid a bird would pick it up and eat it – and would melt. It didn't bear thinking about. I poked at it with a stick, then carefully eased it onto a leaf. It wasn't activated, I knew that, but I wasn't about to touch it. I headed back up the hill, intending to bury it inside the campsite. I was careful not to drop the capsule. And I wouldn't have dropped it, but a stray beam of sunlight hit it and it flashed, and the name engraved on it showed up sharply. *Donnell Urbano.*

That was the capsule I'd dug out of *my* leg. There was still my blood on it. But it wasn't my capsule. Mine had suddenly activated inside Donnell and had killed him. In the back of my mind, an alarm started to ring.

'*Robin, I'm sorry,*' he'd said.

I barely made it inside the perimeter before collapsing. '*En garde,*' I croaked, then I rolled over and stared at the sky. He hadn't been apologizing for not wanting me as a partner. He'd been apologizing for killing me. He hadn't brought anything for filming because he hadn't planned to make a film.

What was going on?

41

Chapter Six

I spent the rest of the day and that night going through Donnell's belongings. What was the most interesting was the portable lab. I had one, but it was nowhere near as advanced as this. His comlink had melted with him. He'd had one of the tattoo links on his wrist. I'd wanted one, but could never afford it. I hadn't really thought about it before. Here was a guy whose parents came from the Still United States of the South as refugees, begging to be let in to the Western State of California with nothing, not even a basic vitapak. Here was a guy who said he was poor, and who worked as a wildlife filmmaker for Tempus U – how had he been able to afford the tattoo comlink? They were *wo cao*, in the awesome sense. You could make it invisible, or call up any design you wanted, or read your mail, check the time, and communicate with your vidcams and your vitapak. Everything appeared on your skin. I'd been desperate to get one. I was going to put it on my wrist and flaunt it. But I'd have to work another ten years and save every credit before I could afford one.

I sifted through his portable lab. Because his comlink was gone, all his notes, papers, bank accounts, and identification were gone too. Tapping my fingernail on my teeth, which I did when I was thinking, and drove Dr Powell crazy, I picked up the only other thing that had survived. His vidcam. Luckily, he hadn't had it on him. Without the comlink, it might not work. On the other hand, we were twelve thousand years away from any kind of techno-guard. In the future, no one could turn on my links or my cams because every attempt by someone not me would set off an alarm. Nothing to trigger the alarm here!

I hit play. A screen appeared. It was your usual home floating screen, with links to different files and hover cams. Nothing said, '*I'm going to try and kill Robin and this is why!*' But there were some files that didn't make sense. Many had the name '*Mars*' in the title, and I knew he liked to go there. But one was called '*Mars trip, family album, Dad's birthday*'. The date was last year. And there was another. Same title. Dated about ten years ago. I frowned. No, twelve thousand years in the future. I was having a hard time situating myself. But Donnell told me his parents died when he was in college.

I opened the first holo, *Mars trip, Dad's birthday*, the one that was ten years old, and my eyes widened. It wasn't Mars. The view was taken from *this* bluff. I studied the scene closer. He'd been here before. *He'd been here before!* My brain went into overdrive.

'Stop,' I said. 'Magnify ten times.' I slid the screen around so I was looking at it and facing the forest where the trees jutted into the meadow. The trees were different. Right now, from where I was sitting, the trees were mature. In Donnell's film, they were saplings. I started the film again and watched as Donnell and five other men built traps near the saplings. Then they baited them. The film must have come from a vidcam set up to capture motion, because suddenly it was night and an animal was heading for the traps.

The cam filmed in infrared, so it was like watching a negative of a film. The animal stayed hidden in the grass until the last minute. Then it surged out of the shadow and swiped its paw at the meat hanging inside the trap, setting off the spring door that slammed shut.

It was a juvenile smilodon. I recognized the shorter teeth – it didn't have the long canines of the adults. The cam showed the men surrounding the cage. I had no idea what they were up to. Donnell stood guard and manned the vidcam. The others were dressed in what I recognized as the protective suits scientists usually wore when they worked with dangerous pathogens. Then went right up to the snarling, spitting beast and shook what I thought were salt and pepper shakers over it. At least, that's what it looked like. I nearly laughed. The men recapped the shakers and moved away. After a while, the cam showed the door opening and the smilodon, the bait in its mouth, leaving the cage.

This happened many more times. The traps got set up in different areas, but all around this bluff. Sometimes there were smilodons and sometimes there were dire wolves. Once there was a huge bear – but it broke out of the cage and left with the bait.

The trapped animals got the salt shaker treatment. I could not figure it out. Most of the animals seemed to be juveniles. The leaves of the trees were turning, soon winter would come. The young had been kicked out of the family groups and were alone, hungry, and fairly easy to trap. Another thing. Something I hadn't noticed. At the foot of the bluff on the river side was a path, and that path led to a cave. Donnell and the men spotted it and had a discussion that Donnell had kept on the recording.

'If it's a paleo-Indian dwelling, we infect the inhabitants. If it's a cave bear, we infect that as well.'

That ended the film. It never specified if there were people or animals in the cave. I did want to find out what the salt and pepper treatment was, so I played the other film. This time it *was* on Mars, near what looked like an office building, and I nearly stopped the film, but then the five men walked into the picture. The picture was not great, but the sound was clear. I had a feeling that Donnell hadn't wanted the men to know he'd been filming them.

'When are you going back again?' one of the men asked. He looked familiar. Perhaps I'd seen him around Tempus U, but I couldn't place him. His face and figure stirred something in my memory. I frowned at the holo.

'Next year. The timing couldn't be better. In this time period, only ten years will have passed. Back in time, it will be more like a century. The animals in the area will all have developed antibodies.' Donnell put his hand out. 'Half the payment now. Half on delivery.'

'One third now. One third when you get back. One third when we develop the vaccine.'

The vid ended there and I stared past the blank screen, towards the river. Donnell had come here and had infected the trapped animals. But it didn't make sense. If the disease was already present back here in this time, why not just come back and get samples?

I shut off the second vid and searched through Donnell's library. There was another Mars vid, called 'A Day at the Zoo'. I turned it on. Again the scene was from the bluff. Donnell had filmed animals. He was, I remembered, a very good wildlife photographer. In the vid, below me, at the river's edge, a group of camels drank. As if reacting to some signal, the small herd raised their heads in unison and walked away. Behind them, on the plain, pronghorns and horses grazed next to glyptodons. A massive bison parted the herds, walking to the river to drink. From the other side of the river came a loud crashing sound as branches broke and bushes were trampled. Out of the spruce forest surged a herd of mammoths. They crowded at the river's edge, holding their trunks high, sniffing the air. The largest male must have had tusks four metres long. They were stained green, from slashing through the underbrush. Its fur was long and matted, its beady eyes glowed amber in the strong sunlight. It gouged the riverbank out, then drank. The largest cow mammoth was next. Not as tall as the bull, and with shorter tusks, she was nonetheless impressive. The other mammoths waited until the lead bull and cow drank, then they crowded into the water. After what seemed like only a short time, the bull mammoth trumpeted, and the herd went crashing back into the forest.

The scene shifted. On the far side of the meadow in the shade of a large tree, a group of smilodons lay in the sun. The adults had huge canines, some nearly thirty centimetres long. There were perhaps twenty big cats. Out of the woods, a pack of dire wolves appeared. They trotted into the sunlight, muzzles lifted, scenting the air. The wolves noticed the smilodons and faded back into the trees. The smilodons ignored them, as they'd ignored the mammoths. That's when the cam zoomed in on the group and I noticed the half-eaten carcass of a *cervalces scotti*, or elk moose. A huge rack of antlers made identification easy.

I paused the vid. There were hardly any animals here. The wolves

I'd seen yesterday were not as large or sleek as the ones in the film. There had been just one glyptodon in the valley. The grass was long, nearly up to my chest. In Donnell's film it had been grazed short. When Donnell had gone back the first time, the animals had been healthy and numerous. Now they were mangy, flea-bitten, and practically all gone. By his reckoning, if I'd understood correctly, he'd been here about a century ago. A hundred years is only about four generations for humans, but it's more like ten or even twenty generations for wolves or big cats. It had taken a century for whatever sickness he'd infected them with to spread. Well, it had worked. It seemed that only a fraction of the animals were left.

I sent my hovercam out and swooped over the whole valley, and over the forest for as far as it ranged. Nothing. The wolves were probably long gone. The glyptodon was the only living thing I spotted in a vast area. Donnell had gone back to infect perfectly healthy animals. Whatever he'd done had worked. What had he sprinkled on the animals? Powder?

The sun set and stars came out. With no pollution and no lights, the stars glittered and shined with a brightness I could never have imagined. I didn't bother leaving my campsite to eat. I opened a quick-meal, ate the tasteless slop, then drank some water. I put my sleeping bag outside and lay down, staring at the incredible sky.

In the middle of the night, I had to get up to pee. According to survival manuals, I should have dug a latrine far from the camp and taken a gun with me. But a quick glance at my floating screen, that I'd set up to capture infrared images, showed nothing around. I put on cropped pants, a light sweater, and running shoes, deactivated my perimeter, and walked down the hill and urinated on the pile of rocks I'd made for Donnell's tomb. I guess I hadn't forgiven him for trying to kill me.

The scientists back in my time had told me to bring warm clothes. A small ice age had supposedly occurred at this time, but right now, the weather was balmy and the ground was dry. It hadn't rained here in a while. The river was high, but not in flood. I thought maybe I'd go fishing tomorrow and see what kinds of fish I could catch. I had studied the megafauna from this time period, and it included some enormous salmon nearly seven feet long. Talk about a meal for a whole tribe.

The night was tranquil but not quiet. The whisper of the breeze in the tall grass and the faint gurgle of the river nearby was a soothing backdrop to the songs of night birds and crickets. There must have been millions of crickets, and their chirping filled the air. Birds, probably owls, hooted, and I thought I heard doves calling. Something splashed in the river, and I spotted a huge, dark shape moving against the current. I thought it might be a giant beaver, so I sent my hovercam over to film. The animal must have sensed it coming, because it dove beneath the dark water before I could identify it.

I had my floating screen with me where I could keep an eye on it. Now I spotted a large animal coming out of the forest. It was the glyptodon. The only one left around here, from what I could see. Perhaps all its kin had died off. I couldn't tell if it was a male or a female, but the cap of armour on the top of its head looked so much like a helmet I started thinking of it as a 'he'.

He shuffled out into the meadow and headed for the river. Out of curiosity, I followed him. He ignored me, so I walked along by his side. We arrived at the river meadow in a companionable silence. He looked at me every now and then, but didn't draw his head in, as he had for the wolves, nor did he threaten me with his massive tail. I stayed well away, but I bent down and tore off handfuls of grass. Jake had taught me this. It was the mark of a herbivore, and would make me appear inoffensive. It seemed to work. The glyptodon walked to the river's edge and drank, and then he nibbled on the tender plants growing in the mud. After a few moments, he turned and went back to the meadow.

The sky was so clear, the stars and moon so bright, that I didn't need my night goggles. I'd put them around my neck, and I had my audio-amplifiers as well, but didn't think I'd need them. My floating screen hovered nearby my shoulder. That gave the glyptodon a pause. Once or twice he stopped grazing and peered at it.

47

I took my time to admire the creature. Its domed carapace, made up of hundreds of interlocking bony plates, was covered with moss on the top and mottled with green and brown. The sides were bare, scraped clean – by grass and branches, I supposed. Its head and tail were covered with long, soft hair, and on the top of its head was that bony plate that looked like a helmet. Its body was pale brownish-grey, and its fur was lighter around its eyes, giving it a surprised look. Its dark eyes were large and had sublimely long white eyelashes. It had a long nose, like a tapir, with which it grasped leaves and plants.

Basically, it looked like a huge turtle, but it was related to the armadillo. The top of its back reached my shoulders. Its head was small, and held about knee-height, giving it a limited range of view. It couldn't pull its head into its shell, like a turtle. But its head was protected by thick armour and two large spikes jutted from its cheeks. When threatened, it thrashed its heavy tail back and forth. The tail was strong enough to break bones, so I imagine most animals kept well away.

Its legs looked too small for its body, but it was spry, and it had long claws on both back and front feet. Supposedly it dug burrows, so I thought it must have a burrow in the forest. I decided I'd find it and photograph it. I knew humans had used its domed carapace for shelters, and one theory for the poor glyptodons' doom was that they had been hunted to extinction. I felt sorry for the creature. It didn't take me for a threat. I sat in the grass, listening to the night-time sounds, and after a while, it walked up to me. I moved away, and it followed. I sat down again, and it edged closer, then snuffled at my foot.

'Hey there, old fellow,' I said softly.

At the sound of my voice it froze. I tensed, ready to spring away if it attacked. It must have weighed two tons and could easily crush me. But instead, it stretched its neck out and patted my foot with its trunk-like nose. Then it snuffled my foot again and licked it.

'Hey,' I giggled. I hadn't bathed, there must be salty sweat on my skin.

The glyptodon finished licking my foot, then went back to grazing. I leaned back in the soft grass and watched it. I was just thinking I should probably get back to camp, when suddenly the glyptodon became agitated. It lifted its head as high as it could and stretched its trunk-like nose out, sniffing loudly. It made a trumpeting noise, and whirled around, as if it couldn't decide where to run.

My floating screen! I'd forgotten to keep checking it. Now, I could see a line of predators coming out of the forest. They were spread apart, encircling the valley and cutting off my retreat to the top of the bluff. I couldn't tell what they were from the image, but I was sure it was the dire wolf pack.

I had three choices. I could jump onto the back of the glyptodon and try to hang on. But the moss on the top of its back would make that nearly impossible. Plus, how to climb up without getting my leg broken by its thrashing tail? It wasn't about to stand still and let me, besides, it could easily toss me off. There was nothing to grasp and hang on to on the round dome.

If I could find the path up the cliff, I might make it to the cave Donnell had spoken about in the film. With a lot of luck, I'd be able to scale the cliff back to my campsite, or I could take a stand inside the cave, but then I'd be trapped. If there were a cave bear inside, I'd be doubly dead.

Or I could jump into the river and take my chance in the swift water. I didn't know what lurked in the river. Giant beavers with huge incisors lived about now, and who knows what kinds of eels or carnivorous fish were in there? Besides, wolves swam and would plunge in after me.

I took option three. I left the glyptodon and ran to the edge of the river, looking for signs of a deep, swift current. I put my night goggles on as I ran, and the landscape jumped into view. A well-worn path ran along the river – probably from centuries of animals walking up and down it. I wasn't really thinking anything as I ran and I didn't have a destination in mind. I set my hovercam and my floating screen to follow me with two quick clicks, and I hit the water running.

Chapter Seven

The river, on the valley side, slowed, widened, and flowed into the meadow so that the water was only about knee-deep for a good fifty yards. Clumps of tall reeds and sawgrass grew in the shallows. I ran and leaped into the water, slipped and slid on mud, grabbed some reeds to keep my footing, and kept running. Behind me, I could hear the glyptodon trumpeting angrily, but a glance at my floating screen showed the wolves simply rushing around it on their way to catch me.

I sprang through the mud and shallow water like a deer, my heart pounding, my breath whistling in my throat. Shoulder-high, knife-edged grass cut through my pants and slashed at my hands and face, but I was so pumped full of adrenaline I could have run through a forest of thorns and not felt anything. My floating screen had been set to stay about eye level, so some of the reeds went right through it, shredding the image now and then. I could still see the dire wolves though. They were grouping together now and gaining on me.

I was thigh-deep now and near panicking. The worst possible scenario was that the water stayed shallow. I surged through the water, but wasn't getting very far or going very fast. Behind me, I heard the wolves splash into the water. I took a huge breath and dove, swimming for the faint line of current I'd spotted. I was a good swimmer, but I was hampered by the reeds and by my clothing. I had no time to take anything off. My night-vision goggles worked fine underwater, and to my relief, I saw the bottom suddenly drop off about three metres away from me.

My lungs were just about to explode when I finally reached the current. A final kick, and I was being swept downstream. I surfaced, gasped for breath, and dared a look behind me. The wolves had stopped where the shallows met the deep water and the current. They stood, chest deep in water, watching me.

I put my head underwater, but silt obscured the water and hampered visibility. I couldn't see the bottom. I floated on my back for a while to rest, but I was starting to get chilled. The current swept me downstream at a steady pace, and I felt confident I'd left the wolves behind, so I began to search the shore for a place to get out.

The cliff soared high above the river, and I saw where it jutted out. That was the bluff with my campsite. My plan was to follow the river's curve and get out where I could make my way up to the camp and the safety of my perimeter. Now, in the middle of the river and in the current, I was having trouble staying afloat. I managed to unfasten my shoes and take them off, watching with regret as they disappeared into the dark. Then I shrugged out of my pants and shirt. I kept them, however. When I got out of the water, I'd put them on again. Clutching my bundle of clothes under one arm, I swam closer to shore, looking at the base of the cliff for a likely spot to land. That's when I noticed a faint path leading up it. I followed the path with my eyes and saw the cave. It was a small one, but clearly a cave, and the only way up to it was a nearly vertical path that looked almost as if someone had hacked footholds into the rock at regular intervals.

The current was speeding up as the river narrowed, pressed between the jutting cliff and the high banks on the opposite side, where the dense spruce forest grew. I kept my eyes on the cave and wasn't looking where I was going. Suddenly, I collided with something large, furry, and muscular. I don't know who was most surprised, me or the giant beaver I'd swum into. It must have been going from one side of the river to the other, and the muddy water had concealed it from me. The water around me exploded as the giant beaver took my presence as an attack, but it didn't try to bite me with its huge teeth, instead it reared up out of the water, twisted its body around, and hit me with its tail.

It missed my face but crashed into my shoulder, numbing my

51

whole arm. I kicked away from it, but it was just as frightened of me and disappeared into the depths. Gasping in pain, I tried to swim one-armed to the shore. The blow had stunned me. My adrenaline was wearing off, and I started to shiver and feel light-headed. Then I realized I'd lost my clothing.

I ducked my head underwater and peered around. The water was deep, the current swift, and there was no sign of pants or shirt. Suddenly I saw a massive body covered with silver scales surge out of the murk and head straight towards me. It was a nightmare fish, nearly three metres long, with two spiked teeth on the tip of its narrow, jutting jaw. Its eyes glowed blood red in the penumbra. I flailed to the surface and back-paddled, desperate to get out of the water now. But the fish had no interest in me. It brushed past me as if it didn't even see me, heading upstream. I saw more fish then, all swimming with single-minded determination up the river. I recognized them as the sabertooth salmon, probably heading to their mating grounds. I let my breath out in shaky relief, and my heart stopped pounding so hard.

But where there are salmon, there are bears. Another shiver ran through me and I kicked harder towards the riverbank. My injured arm dragged me down and I struggled to keep my face out of the water to breathe, but I'd reached shallower water and, thankfully, my feet touched the bottom. Trees leaned over the river, and I wasn't keen on getting out here. Trees were where the big cats liked to hang out, and trees could conceal other animals. But I had no choice. I felt sick. The beaver had hurt me and I needed to get my vitapak and find out how badly I'd been injured.

My strength was ebbing rapidly, and the current was still strong, trying to push me downstream. I grabbed hold of some roots with my good hand and held on. Carefully pulling myself in with the roots and fighting the current all the way, I approached the shore, looking for a way to climb out. Then I saw an area where a rock-slide had fallen into the water. I let go of the roots and managed to crawl onto a large, flat boulder – this time the current was a help more than a hindrance, pushing me up onto the rock. I lay on my stomach, panting, trying to clear my head. If I could get to the shore here, there might be a path around the base of the cliff, and I could find my way back to my camp. I couldn't climb, that was sure. My left arm hurt abominably, the slightest movement made me want to scream.

At least four metres separated me from dry land, but it may as well have been four hundred. I tried to get up to a crouch, but slid back onto the rock, my body wracked with tremors.

'No, get up, Robin. Get up! Keep your eyes open!' I spoke sternly to myself, hoping the sound of my own voice would help. It didn't. I couldn't stop shaking, and my head throbbed. The water on the river shimmered and sparkled, the sharp points of light blinding me. I unhooked my night-vision goggles and tore them off. The glowing, lime green surroundings faded to monochrome greys. The moon was full though, and that light on the water had been too much for my night-vision settings. I fumbled at the strap, meaning to turn it down, but my fingers were clumsy and stiff; the goggles slipped out of my grasp and fell into the water.

'No!' I grabbed at them, but a blinding pain shot through me. Gasping, nearly fainting, I lay back down on the rock.

'Yasmine,' I groaned, feeling my conscience slipping away. 'You told me to call you . . . Oh, *ta ma de*, Yasmine, I'm losing my mind.' But it felt good to call her. Like she wasn't twelve thousand years away, not even born yet. Hadn't died yet either. I raised my voice to the sky. 'Yasmine!'

Most people, I thought wryly, called their mothers when they were dying. I'd never called my mother. I'd never called her, and I never would. My father killed her then committed suicide in front of me when I was only nine. I could never remember that day. No matter how hard the psychologists probed or the psychiatrists prodded – with drugs, with therapy, with hypnosis, or with electric shocks – nothing ever brought back that memory.

I wished I could remember something, anything about her, but there was a blank spot in my mind where she should have been. I don't remember the good, I don't remember the bad. But I wished, at that moment, I could remember her just a little. Instead, I sobbed Yasmine's name, over and over, until everything went dark.

They say that when you die, your life flashes before your eyes. I wonder who said that, and if it's been scientifically proven. If I had been taking part in the study, I'd say that no – nothing flashes before your eyes. Everything went dark, and then things turned grey.

I heard a familiar name. The rescue team found me, I thought, and struggled to open my eyes. But why were they saying *Yasmine*? I still hurt. My body shook as tremors of pain wracked it, but help was on its way! I blinked, trying to focus. The scene wavered strangely, and a sharp, musky odour assailed me. Things came to me bit by bit – I lay on something hard, yet soft. I wasn't outside, I was in some sort of . . . tent? The walls kept wavering. I couldn't see the roof. I tried to sit, but when I moved my arm, a violent, grinding pain shot through me.

I gasped, but the pain had shocked me awake. I rolled over onto my good side and crouched, bracing myself with my arm. I was naked, and I lay on something fuzzy. A fur rug? I shook my head and moaned when the pain flared again. I tried to concentrate on the fur. Deep fur. I dug my fingers into it and tried to clear my head. I must have been dreaming.

'Yasmine.'

I hadn't dreamed it. Someone was calling my friend's name. The walls kept wavering, but I understood now. Fire. A fire flickered, and I had been lying in front of it. Was I back at my campsite? Where was I? The walls wavered and I tilted forward. Now I was on my knees, one hand on the fur with my arm braced to keep me from falling, and my wounded arm cradled in my lap. I steadied myself and looked around. A cave. I was in a cave.

My mind kept stopping and starting, I saw things in flashes. A man. Sitting cross-legged in front of me. Copper skin. Light brown eyes. A worried expression on his face. Bare arms with strange tattoos. Leather leggings tied on with leather thongs. Long hair tied back with what looked like plaited reeds.

54

He ducked his head down, his eyes level with mine. Tentatively, he said, 'Yasmine?' In his hand, he held a short lance made of wood, its tip sharpened and blackened by fire. Or could it be blood? I squinted at the spear and tried to get my brain to work.

'How-how do you know my friend's name?' I asked.

He bared his teeth, showing a gap where an incisor was missing. I don't know what he said, but it sounded like *Hashdonnaynij*, and was clearly a question. I grimaced and shook my head once. More slowly, he said, '*Hash donnay nij? Hash na nina?*'

'I'm hurt. I need to get back to my campsite. The wolves chased me.' I paused, then gave a deep howl, like a wolf, and said, 'Wolf.' I howled again and said, 'Wolf!'

His eyes widened. '*Makii*,' he said. He pointed his fingers into triangle ears and gave a life-like howl. '*Makii hohoy!*' he pointed at me with his spear and then poked me with it. '*Ni nabi to azehn hagi makii adin?*'

I didn't understand any of that, but figured *makii* meant dire wolf. I didn't like the spear though, and I cringed. He gave a snort and put it down. He stared at me intently. I couldn't read his expression. I was afraid to smile, in case it was a sign of aggression. I didn't know what signals he was waiting for. Did a nod mean 'yes', or 'no'? If I looked at him, was that bad or good? I kept my gaze on his though. He looked straight at me, not averting his eyes. He wasn't acting hostile, or so I hoped.

'Makii?' I said, hesitantly.

He howled, scaring me, but he wasn't shoving a pointy stick at my chest anymore. We were getting somewhere. Now to tell him I had to get to the top of the hill, where I could heal my arm with my vitapak. Wolf was easy. How to explain a vitapak to a caveman? And how did he know Yasmine's name?

I lay back down again. Sickness rolled over me in waves, but my memory was coming back. I'd crawled up on a rock and called Yasmine's name. That was it. The caveman must have heard me, and thought that was my name. I closed my eyes. In a minute, I'd tell him. I'd explain. I'd . . .

55

Chapter Eight

When I next opened my eyes, sunlight slanted into the cave. Motes of dust danced and sparkled in the air. An acrid, bittersweet odour filled my nostrils, and smoke made lazy spirals in the breeze. I heard a crackling sound, but it was just the fire dying into embers. My bed, if you can call a pile of furs a bed, faced the cave entrance with the fire between me and the opening. The cave was little more than an indentation in the rock, and not deep at all. It hadn't been lived in long. The fire had hardly any ash. There were no other signs of human presence except the bed of furs and the fire. I would have expected a more structured space, perhaps some baskets, articles of clothing, weapons even.

I started to feel better and sat up, being careful not to jog my arm. I needed to urinate again, so, bracing myself on the stone wall, I stood. My knees wobbled, but I was up. I checked, and saw my comlink was still around my wrist. I called up my vidcam. It flew into the cave like a demented bat, and I winced. It must have spent the night outside and gotten hung up in a tree. A small branch was stuck to it.

I plucked the branch off it and sent it out to scout, and then I opened a floating screen. I didn't want to walk into danger. If I had to, I'd stay here until the rescue team came and have my vidcam lead them to me. The screen showed the river. And it also showed the cave I was in. It wasn't the cave I'd seen from the river – no, that one had been high on the cliff. This one was nearly flush with the river and must flood after too much rain. No wonder it wasn't used as a dwelling. The caveman must have dragged me here from the river and lit the fire for me. And he'd gotten furs for me. His intentions had been good. He'd gone out of his way to help me. Another thought occurred. I hadn't been wearing my modern clothes. There wasn't too much about me that screamed '*Woman From the Future!*'. My comlink was one I'd chosen because it looked so natural – the band looked like leather with three large copper beads on it: one for my floating screen, one for my vidcam, and one for my computer.

I floated my screen in front of me and sent the vidcam downriver looking for the caveman. There he was, trudging along with a pile of sticks on his shoulder, dragging some sort of dead animal behind him. *Oh joy. Breakfast.*

My vidcam didn't bother him. It actually looked and sounded like a large insect. I sent it up high in order to see the lay of the land and scout out my campsite. I'd judged correctly. I was on the right side of the river and I could reach the camp easily – maybe a three-hour hike in my wounded state. Everything in the campsite seemed untouched. I set the perimeter by distance command. Then I sent the vidcam to its power base. I shut off my floating screen, and tried to figure out which of the furs I could borrow to use as a towel.

I grabbed a small rabbit skin, hoping the caveman wouldn't mind. I hated calling him that, but I thought Paleo-Indian was too long, and we weren't in India, and I was having trouble concentrating enough to figure out a better name. I shuffled out of the cave and blinked in the strong sunlight. It was still early, but the mist had already dissipated and there was a dry, dusty smell in the air. The cliff rose behind me, and in front of me, the rockslide had cleared a space down to the river. I recognized the boulder I'd lain on when I'd dragged myself out of the water.

Carefully, I picked my way to the river's edge and relieved myself. Then I used the skin to wash with, dipping it in the water and rubbing my legs and body. I splashed water on my face, and wished I had something to bind my arm. Every time I moved, it caused me severe pain. A willow tree leaned over the water, and I broke off a few trailing branches. I squatted on a flat rock and started winding the branches around my neck and chest, braiding more in as I went, to make a sort of sling/cradle for my arm. The willow branches were long, thin, and flexible enough to be perfect for the job. When I finished, I stood and saw the caveman had arrived.

I clambered back to the cave entrance, put the rabbit skin on a rock to dry, and watched as he dumped his pile of sticks on the fire, then tossed the dead animal on top. I grimaced. Gourmet cooking hadn't been invented yet. He had barely peeled the skin off the beast – whatever it was. It was hard to tell, it had already been eaten by something else, I think. The head and most of the body were missing. Only a chewed-up haunch remained.

I pointed at it.

'N'akacha,' said the man.

I had no idea if that meant food, fire, sticks, meat, or whatever animal it had been. But I repeated it. 'N'akacha?' I made it a question by putting an upward inflection on the word.

He didn't respond at first, making me wonder if inflection was part of his language. He hesitated, then said, 'Ee n'akacha.'

Interesting. He'd added an 'ee' sound. In linguistics, that sound was associated with the word 'small' in hundreds of unrelated languages. Whatever a n'akacha was, this was a small one then. A baby? I put my hand close to the floor of the cave and said, 'Ee?'

The man tilted his head, as if listening, but didn't react. Instead, he touched the sling I'd fixed up for my arm and made a grunting sound. Then he turned back to the fire and put some branches back in that had fallen out. So much for the conversation. I surreptitiously opened my comlink and took some pictures of him. He was short, by modern standards, but so was I. In fact, we looked like we could be related, except he was very muscular and his nose was crooked – whether by birth or by accident, it was hard to tell. His skin was tanned by the sun and wind. His hair was black with threads of grey. It was long, but not straight. It had a definite curl to it, like mine. Mine was cut short though, in what I called 'a cap of curls'. He had deep-set light brown eyes, broad cheekbones, a strong chin, and large teeth. Like most people who'd come to the Americas over the land passage from Asia, he had hardly any hair on his face and none on his body.

He wore leggings that resembled chaps made of what looked like rabbit skin, and his penis was covered by a flap of cured leather tied to his waist by a braided leather belt. The leather flap was wide, and I supposed it protected his tender parts when he walked through tall grass or brush.

His leggings were held up by narrow thongs, and along the sides, long quills had been poked into the seams in a decorative pattern. His feet were bare, but on his ankles and inside his big toe were calluses that made me think he often wrapped his feet in leather fastened with thongs. He'd tied his hair back with strips of leather to keep it out of his eyes. Apart from the decorative quills, his clothing was rough and unadorned. But his arms and torso were covered with tattoos. I was fascinated. Around this time, twelve thousand years ago, mankind had been decorating cave walls with paintings, carving statues in bone and stone, stringing shells into jewellery, and drawing tattoos on their bodies. His tattoos were symbols, but I recognized one. I drew my breath in with a low whistle.

He whirled around, looking out the cave entrance. I jumped. I hadn't expected that a whistle meant danger, but that is what it seemed to mean. He peered out, then looked at me. An expression, the first I'd seen, crossed his face. But I had no idea what that expression meant. It looked — and I suddenly got it. He'd been frightened. He must live on the very edge of fear every second of the day. Embarrassed, I pointed to the tattoo on his shoulder. It was stylized, but instantly recognizable. A smilodon.

He touched his arm and pointed, and I saw a wicked scar. 'Nashdotso,' he said. 'Atte jay nashdotso, shi shay, ish ke lineedah.'

My linguistics classes taught that some words and sounds were universal. The nose, for example, had the 'n' sound in nearly every single language on earth. Mother had the 'm' sound. And here was that 'ee' sound again. Perhaps he'd said he had been attacked by a smilodon when he was young. 'Lineedah?' I inflected it as a question, and held my hand low to the ground.

'*Ahoh.*' He peered at me, then pointed at my chest. '*Ha'ee.*' He took my good hand. I flinched, but he didn't pull me closer. He held my hand and rubbed it with his thumb. Then he touched my knees, and my feet, all of which were badly scratched by my struggles in the river and on the rocks.

Ahoh. That might be 'yes'. And *ha'ee.* The *ee* sound. Young. Small. He thought I was young. I confused him. I could see that. My skin was smooth, my hands soft, my skin was tender. To him, I must look and feel like a newborn, except I was as tall as he was. And I was soft. I might be fit for my time period; compared to him, I was weak and fat. Not chubby – but fat plumped my skin and smoothed my cheeks. He didn't have any fat – his skin hugged his muscles, bones, and tendons, and his skin was weather-worn, scarred, and tough.

I grimaced and glanced outside. The sun was climbing higher. Soon it would be midday. I wanted to be gone before then. I had to intercept the rescue team and make sure they didn't find this cave man – this man – did he have a name?

I pulled my hand from his grip and pointed to his tattoo. '*Nash-dotso,*' I said. I howled and said, '*Makii.*' Then I pointed to myself and said, 'Robin.' I insisted, pointing again, and saying 'Robin.' Then I pointed at him.

He looked at my finger, and his eyebrows knitted together in concentration. He took my hand and put it on his chest. I felt his heart beating. '*Yah.*' He pushed my hand harder, as if he wanted to imprint my hand on his skin. 'Yah,' he repeated.

My skin prickled. 'Yah?'

He let go of my hand and went back to tending the fire. I closed my eyes. His name was Yah. When he heard me calling for my friend, Yasmine, he had heard his name. He'd come because I'd called him. A shiver of some indescribable emotion ran over me. 'Thank you, Yasmine,' I whispered.

Yah was poking about in the fire, so I pulled my fur bed apart and looked for something to wear. A long, wide strip of soft leather had been bundled up. I unfolded it and wrapped it around my hips. It

60

was awkward with one hand, but I managed to knot it on the side. It made a rough miniskirt. Fashion in the Stone Age. I wish I had some quills like Yah had on his leggings to decorate it.

Yah came back. He paused when he saw my skirt and grunted. Then he held a piece of meat and offered it to me. '*Tah al.* Robin, *bi tah al.*'

He was giving me the first bite. He was inviting me to eat with him. We were friends. We sat and ate whatever it was – I still had no idea what kind of animal I was gnawing on, but it was pretty good, in a meaty, much too rare, cooked with its skin on directly in the fire and with no salt way – well, I was starving.

Afterwards, I felt better and wanted to thank him. 'Thank you, Yah,' I said. I put my hands together and bowed, hoping the sign of respect and thanks that existed in my time had existed through the ages. Then I turned to leave.

He blocked my way, took my hand and pointed up the cliff. 'Robin *ako nee dish* Yah.'

I looked in the direction he pointed, and saw the entrance to the cave I'd seen from the river. He pointed again, then pointed at him and at me. His meaning was clear. 'I don't think I can climb up there,' I said.

He shook my hand and pulled at it again. '*Ako nee dish.*'

I pointed to my injured arm, but he tugged at my hand then picked up his spear and walked away, turning to make sure I followed. With a sigh, I set off after him.

He pointed with his spear, showing me a path along the edge of the river. We passed through a copse of tall trees, then the path took a hard turn and led to the base of the cliff. But as I'd noticed from the river, hand and footholds had been carved into the rock, and in fact it was as easy as walking up a steep staircase. A very steep, very high staircase. At one point I looked down, and the drop was dizzying. But the view was terrific. I paused. I couldn't see the meadow from here, but my base camp must be nearly directly overhead. I could see up and down the river though, and the forest on the far side all the way to what looked like low, purple mountains. A bird sailed in the sky. It veered closer, and my heart nearly stopped. It was gigantic, easily big enough to grab me, and if not carry me off, at least knock me off the cliff. Whistling frantically, I scrambled up the rest of the stairs and flung myself into the cave.

Yah pushed me behind him and waved his spear at the sky, yelling loudly.

The bird flew past the cave entrance, so close I could see the glint in its yellow eyes. It was an *Argentavis*, with a seven-metre wingspan and a long, wicked beak. It banked, then sailed into the sky. Sunlight glinted off its feathers. It had looked black, but when the sun hit it, glints of gold and blue appeared, like sparks running up and down its wings.

Yah stood in the entrance until the bird disappeared, then he shook his spear once again and gave a piercing yell at the empty sky. I turned away from him and looked into the cave. This was where he lived. Along the walls were baskets woven from bark, willow branches, and reeds. A thicket of spears leaned against one wall. A pile of furs formed a sort of bench. My nose was assaulted by hundreds of strong odours. Tanned skins. Cured leather. Old smoke from blackened tree branches in a huge stone hearth in the middle of the floor. The smells were from loam, moss, something acrid, something fishy, charcoal, grilled meat, pine pitch, and there was an underlying smell of something sickeningly sweet. The hair on my arms prickled. I knew that smell. Sickness. Death. Rotting flesh.

My eyes grew accustomed to the gloom, and then I saw them. In the back. On a pallet. Two people. But not asleep. They were dead. I was frightened, but not panicked. I wasn't afraid for my life. Yah was standing next to them, his head bowed. He no longer held his spear. He didn't look threatening. He was mourning. Those two had been precious to him. I came closer. He looked at me and patted his own arm. Another age-old gesture. *I'm sorry.* I had the impression he was telling me he was sad. I nodded and patted his shoulder gently.

The bodies were of a woman and a very young girl. Then I saw there were three. A baby as well. Nestled in the woman's arms. They had been dead for a while.

62

He turned to me. 'Yah', he said, pointing to himself. Then he knelt by the woman's body, stroked her hair, and said, 'Mesha. *Mesha*,' he insisted, then pointed to himself, then the woman. 'Yah. Mesha *Yah mi*.'

He was telling me that the dead woman had been Mesha, his woman. Mesha Yah *mi*. Mesha, who belonged to Yah. He pointed to the two other bodies. To the girl and the infant. 'Na Yah *mi*. Ehba Yah *mi*.' His children, Na and Ehba.

His pain was a palpable thing. He tried to stand straight, but sorrow bent him over.

'*Adeez*,' he said, his voice breaking. He rubbed his eyes hard and drew a deep breath. He pointed to me. '*Adeez? Aki?*' He pointed out the cave, his expression quizzical, but I didn't know what he was trying to say. Names I could understand, but not the rest. He pointed to me again, then outside. I thought he was probably asking where my people were.

I pointed to myself and held up one finger. I was alone. He didn't seem to understand what I was trying to convey. I tried again. I pointed to him, and to the dead bodies. I held up one finger for each, pointing and adding a finger. One, two, three, four. I showed him four fingers and indicated him and his family. Then I pointed to myself and held up one finger again.

He held up one finger, imitating me. But I don't know if he understood the concept of counting. I shrugged. It wasn't important. What was important was me getting back to my campsite and getting my vitapak to scan my arm. I was almost sure I'd dislocated it. As long as I held it still, the pain stayed bearable. Another thing that was important. I had to examine Yah's family. I wasn't sure how close I could get to the bodies, but I needed to know how and why they died.

I opened my comlink. It would work without him noticing. From what I could see, they had been sort of preserved by soaking in some liquid – I sniffed. Tar, yes. There was definitely a strong whiff of tar. And tannin. Perhaps a bath of oak chips? Pine pitch, definitely. Bands of leather were wrapped around their bodies and were attached to several branches, holding their arms and legs straight. Then I saw the pallet they were lying on was carefully arranged. It was made of wood, and the branches were stacked carefully, leaving no doubt that this was a funeral pyre.

Why hadn't he burned them yet? I thought about it. Maybe he'd been meaning to burn them, but he wasn't ready yet. Maybe he was going to do it, then he'd found me. Or he planned on waiting. His tribe was gone – and these three were the last to go – leaving him. He couldn't bear to be alone. I had no idea, actually, why he hadn't lit the pyre yet. All my thoughts were just conjecture. As he sat near his wife, his hand on her head, murmuring, I recorded some close-ups of the bodies with my comlink, holding my wrist near their bodies as discreetly as possible, then I uploaded the images to my vidcam to examine later. Then, because I didn't know what else to do, I went back down the steps (after checking to make sure there were no giant vultures flying around).

I thought Yah would stay in his cave with his family, and I was surprised to see him climbing down and starting to follow me. But if the rescue team showed up and found him, they would probably eliminate him. Already I was breaking I don't know how many laws. I tried to tell him to go back. Mostly because I wanted to switch on my floating screen to see if the way to my camp was clear. I pointed to the top of the cliff, then to me.

'I have to go up there,' I said. My arm hurt. When I walked I jarred it, and I was still weak and tired. I had to leave now, before evening came. 'I'm afraid of the *makii*,' I explained, although I knew he couldn't understand. I pointed to his tattoo. 'And I need to find a sabre-toothed tiger. A smilodon. I screwed up my eyes, trying to remember the word. 'Nah – nash something.'

Yah snorted. Again, I couldn't tell if he was amused or angry. The social signals I knew were missing. '*Nashdotso*,' he said, and then held out his hand. He hesitated, then put one finger up and pointed to his tattoo. Then he showed me one finger. To make his point, he put his hand on my chest, over my heart, and said 'Robin.' Then held one finger. And then 'Yah,' and held up two fingers. Then, one finger pointed to his tattoo, and only one finger held up. There were two of us. And one smilodon. He knew where one was.

So much for him not understanding the concept of counting. Humans had probably counted on their fingers ever since they started communicating with each other. Some historians insisted that maths and writing had evolved around the same time, but this was a good five thousand years before writing would emerge. I had a sudden thought that maybe no one had counted before, and here I was, teaching someone to count, and history would be totally changed, and the Time Senders would have a *putain* meltdown trying to figure out where everything went wrong, and I'd probably get back and get fired.

I started laughing then, and couldn't stop. Yah didn't get it, so he just stood, looking around, sniffing the air. I finally got a hold of myself. Three hours, I thought to myself. Then I crawl into my tent, set my perimeter, and give myself a good dose of painkiller. I was looking forward to that painkiller. I started down the path, keeping close to the river. Yah walked at my heels, but my brain was too fractured to tell him to leave me alone.

As we walked, he didn't say anything, but I noticed he made signs with his hands now and then. I started paying attention. When he caught me looking at him, he made the signs again. Then again. I had no idea what they could mean. *Nice day for a walk? Where are you going? Are you out of your fractured mind?* I shook my head, but that didn't seem to mean anything to him. Our communication was limited to names, the numbers one and two, and that was it. We couldn't convey emotions, ideas, or the past and the future. We were in the here and now, and only a tenuous bond held us together. I thought he probably stayed with me from a sort of clan instinct. Again, it helped that I resembled him physically. If I'd been wearing my clothes, it would have alienated him. As it was, he was nearly naked, and I was naked except for the strip of leather I'd knotted around my hips and the willow branch sling around my neck and chest.

The meadow came into view. I stopped and scanned it, but there was no sign of the glyptodon or the wolves. In the distance, halfway up the hill, I could see the pile of rocks I'd left on that *bang wa* Donnell's grave. My camp was out of sight on the top of the hill behind some large boulders. I started walking into the meadow, but Yah grabbed my good arm and stopped me. He was agitated, and before I knew what was happening, he threw me down and rolled over me, pinning me to the ground.

At first, the pain in my arm nearly blinded me. It hurt so much I couldn't even scream. I gasped, tears poured down my face, and I whimpered. Then panic hit me. What was Yah doing? Was he going to rape me? For some reason, this calmed me down. I was trained in self-defence, as soon as the agony wore off, I would make him regret being born.

But he wasn't raping me. He pressed his hand over my mouth and slowly got to his knees. He looked, then crouched down again. His expression didn't change, but I could feel his heart pounding. I looked at him and forced my muscles to relax. He made an 'O' with his mouth and whistled softly. That sound meant danger. After, he took his hand off my mouth. I was quiet. Slowly, he pointed to his tattoo. The one of the sabre-toothed tiger. He pointed at the tattoo, then pointed towards the forest, on the other side of the meadow.

I couldn't hear anything except insects buzzing, the wind in the grass, and Yah's quiet breathing. But he was breathing fast, and his heart rate was elevated. He stayed in a low crouch, his spear held tightly, his muscles trembling with tension.

I hated not being able to see anything. Carefully, I rolled over, paused to let waves of pain wash over me, then pulled my legs in, crouching next to Yah. I retched a few times, nausea twisting my gut. When my head cleared and my nausea diminished, I tapped my comlink and called my vidcam. In a few moments, it arrived, buzzing loudly. Yah barely glanced at it. Then I activated my floating screen, and he fell over backwards.

He didn't made a sound, but he jabbed it with his spear, backing up frantically, grabbing at my leg and trying to pull me with him. The spear was messing with the screen, so I floated it higher, and sent the vidcam to scan for wildlife. If there was a sabre-toothed tiger around, at least this way we could see it coming. That was, if I could calm Yah down enough to look at the picture.

I pulled away from him and patted his leg. I patted my leg, patted my chest, and pointed to the floating screen and to my eyes. Then I pointed to his tattoo. He wasn't happy. He was about two seconds away from leaping up and running. I wanted to calm him, but then the tiger appeared on the screen. It was on the edge of the forest, lying in a patch of sunlight between two large trees.

My breath caught in my throat. It was magnificent. Fantastic. Unbelievable. Its copper coat glowed in the sun. Black mottled spots, looking almost like large rosettes, covered its back and sides. Its legs had tiger stripes on them. It had a short tail tufted with pale yellow fur. The hair inside its large black ears was yellow too, but its huge canines were what really caught my eye. They gleamed like ivory. They looked so out of place to me – they made the animal seem more exotic than the huge dire wolves or the vulture, or even the sabretooth salmon. This big cat somehow stood out. Its teeth were strange yet wonderful. And deadly. I peered closer.

A hole suddenly appeared in the screen. Yah had thrown his spear at it. The image wavered, and the motion alerted the tiger. It raised its head and looked in our direction. No time to explain. We were out of sight, and hopefully the tiger couldn't hear or smell us. Staying low, I crept up the hill towards my camp. If I could make it to the perimeter, I'd be safe.

I pushed through the tall grass, keeping an eye on the screen. I must have made a loud rustling in the grass. The sabre-toothed tiger stood and pricked its ears. I started running. I passed the pile of stones and headed uphill. Behind me, I could see the tiger starting to run as well. It had spotted me, and now I was its prey.

My arm hindered me, of course, but I could still run fast. So could Yah, he was running with me, but staying just behind me. He'd picked up his spear, I noticed. We passed the first boulder. The cat was gaining. My perimeter was just ahead. I deactivated it. We were going to make it. And then the other boulder, the one nearest the perimeter, got up and moved. It was the glyptodon. I screamed, because I couldn't dodge, and I ran smack into its armoured hide. It swiped its tail at me, but Yah was there, and managed to push me away. The tail caught him on the leg and he screamed, his leg buckling under him.

We were both screaming, the glyptodon was trumpeting, and the sabre-toothed tiger suddenly bounded up the hill and launched itself at me.

Chapter Nine

The glyptodon went berserk. Being crashed into by a human had startled it, but the tiger leaping into its sight was too much. It whirled around and swung its tail in a mighty arc. The tiger dodged, and I rushed in, grabbed Yah, and dragged him towards my perimeter. If only I could make it! Safety was just on the other side of the trumpeting, stomping glyptodon. The sabre-toothed tiger ignored the glyptodon. Thinking we were trapped, it paused its attack and climbed onto a boulder. If I remembered what Jake had said, it would next leap onto its prey (me) and stab it (me again) with its huge canines. Jake also said the big cats could easily jump ten metres. I was only about two metres away from it, so close I could smell it, so close I could sense the heat of its body. In despair, I froze, staring at my doom. I did not want to get stabbed by those terrifying teeth.

Two things saved me: male ego and my floating screen. On top of the rock, the smilodon, a male, suddenly decided to mark its territory. It probably thought I was a foregone conclusion – and he was already making sure no rivals would steal my carcass. He raised his tail and sprayed a jet of urine all over, hitting me.

'That is disgusting,' I screamed, but that gave me time to get my floating screen ready.

The smilodon bunched its muscles, ready to pounce, and I sent my floating screen straight at its head. Surprised, the huge cat swiped at it with its paw. The screen shredded like mist, and then reformed. I turned the vidcam to film me and sent the screen towards the cat again, making the screen as big as it would go, life-sized, so that now the cat thought I was running away. The smilodon jumped at the screen, passing straight through it. He whirled around, and started chasing the screen.

I dashed around the glyptodon and saw Yah, still lying on the ground, out cold. I grabbed his wrist with my good hand and pulled with all my remaining strength. Crying, and gasping in pain and fright, I stumbled into the safety perimeter, dragging Yah after me. '*En garde!*' I shouted, and the perimeter lit up in a shower of sparks, as the glyptodon blundered into it. 'No! Go away!' I waved my arm but the huge creature was now inside the perimeter and trampling all over my campsite. Suddenly, it froze. In front of my tent. My large, beige, domed tent. A minute went by. Outside the perimeter, the sabre-toothed tiger had disappeared, following my floating screen that I'd sent down into the valley. Inside my perimeter, the glyptodon stretched its head as far as it could go and trumpeted softly. I started to laugh then, and cry at the same time. The poor beast thought my tent was another glyptodon.

I left the lovesick glyptodon cooing at my tent and bent over Yah. He was in bad shape. His leg looked like it had been badly broken and he had a huge bruise on his chest. I thought maybe a few of his ribs might be cracked. My supplies had been scattered all over by the glyptodon, but I found my vitapak. First things first. One-handed, I took a large sterile gauze pad and wiped the smilodon urine off me and put it in a sample bag. After that, I gave myself a dose of pain-killer and carefully unwrapped the willow branches from my chest, freeing my arm. Then I scanned my shoulder. I had a dislocation of the glenohumeral joint and an acromioclavicular joint separation – in other words, my arm was out of its socket, and my collarbone had also been displaced. I'd have to realign my arm, put my joints back in place, and then put a cast on everything to hold it still. The glyptodon was still mooing softly at my tent, and my medbot was inside. Yah woke up, screamed, and fainted again. Far away, from the forest, came an echoing screech. The smilodon? A giant vulture? I'd really been looking forward to some peace and quiet.

I sighed, and went to the tent. The glyptodon ignored me, so I quickly stepped inside and grabbed the medbot and my second perimeter fencing. I sent up a perimeter around Yah and me, and deactivated the outer perimeter, so the glyptodon could leave when it finished courting my tent. Then I got busy working on my arm. Actually, the medbot got to work. I turned it on, then sat still as it moved over me like a giant spider. I was used to it, but I thought Yah would suffer an attack if he saw it, so I used one of my sleep jabs on him to make sure he stayed passed out.

The medbot straightened my arm, then used needles to pin everything together. Some needles went into my body then melted into my bones, and others found my torn muscles, tendons, and ligaments, healing and soothing them at the same time. The medbot then spun a cast over my shoulder and arm. It chirped and clicked as it worked, and when the red lights on its top turned green, it meant the program had finished.

I programmed it for another operation, and sent it over to Yah. The medbot whirred, probed, and took blood samples, and red lights flashed everywhere. I tapped my comlink and called my floating screen back from where it had been acting as a lure to the smilodon. The screen appeared in front of me and I sent the medbot's analysis to it. When the results came back, they gave me a pause.

'So that's what Donnell was doing,' I said, looking at Yah's sleeping form. 'He was coming back to get antibodies. Your blood is full of them. Your woman and your children died, but you survived. You caught the Typhus-77, but you survived. How did he infect everyone, though?' I thought, absent-mindedly scratching my leg. Suddenly I swore. Scratching. Fleas. Not powder. The salt shakers must have been full of fleas. The men wearing the protective clothing had shaken infected fleas over the captured animals. Donnell and his partners had developed a deadly new typhus-type disease. They had probably done it in one of the labs on Mars, using the ancient feline typhus. A terribly dangerous virus, it had a short incubation period and a near one hundred per cent fatality rate if untreated. It was also terribly resistant, being able to survive for months, even years, outside a host body. Using their man-made virus, Donnell had gone

71

back in time with the men and they'd infected this whole area. Then they'd returned and set the disease loose on Earth.

I closed the tent flap and sat down next to Yah. The air was cool, but the sky remained clear. I wondered if this was a drought, and made a note to look at Donnell's tapes again and compare water levels in the river. I was tired, but despite the painkillers the medbot had given me, my arm and shoulder still ached.

I hesitated, then called up my floating screen and a holo of Yasmine. This was one of the first ones we'd done. She sat in a chair near a window, and I could see rain streaming down the glass panes. She reached out and tapped the window, and the glass darkened. 'I hate the rain,' she said with a frown. 'I want it to be sunny.'

'You want to talk about the weather?' my voice came from behind the screen.

She ignored me. 'My mother came yesterday. She asked about you.' Yasmine sighed. '*Promise* me you'll call her. I know my father lives on another plane of consciousness – he's hopeless when it comes to the real world. He'll probably be able to contact me on "the other side". And my brothers are twins. They'll support each other. But my mom will need someone, and I hope it will be you.'

'I'm not very good with mothers.' My voice again, coming from beyond.

Yasmine put her finger to her lips. 'No talking. Just me. You can answer back later – when I'm gone. Right now I'm asking you please, make sure you call my mother. If she hangs up on you, call back. Send holos of yourself. Write notes. She'll never admit it, but she'll need you.'

'I need you.' This time Yasmine reached behind her and took her pillow, and threw it at me. It disappeared when it reached my floating screen, but I ducked anyhow.

I turned off the holo. I'd tried to call her mother, and she'd been distant and unfriendly. She hadn't hung up, but she'd made it clear I was no longer part of their family group. I'd tried once more, and this time I'd gotten her answering service. She'd never called back.

Yasmine's twin brothers came to visit me one day, and I sent a note to her father, who was a professor of ancient literature and a philosopher. He wrote back with a poem I could never understand. Then they politely closed the doors between us. I didn't try to contact them after that, although I kept the poem her father sent me. One day I'd ask him what it meant. Probably when we met in the afterlife somewhere.

I cupped my chin in my hand and watched while the medbot fixed Yah's chest (three broken ribs, a punctured lung) then worked over his leg (a broken femur). The medbot spun a gorgeous shimmery rainbow cast on his leg, and I had no idea how I was going to explain *that* to Yah. I'd had fun programming my medbot, and one of the programs had been *artistic casts*. (I never thought I'd actually need one). My arm was encased in glittery black and white zebra stripes. The cast would hold until the bone knitted, then dissolve on its own.

The medbot shot Yah up with antibiotics and all the vaccines he'd missed by being born in the Pleistocene period. And his blood was worth a fortune. If I took some back to my time, to the future, I could sell it to the governments all over the world. I'd be rich beyond dreams. Which was what that *sha bi* Donnell had wanted. But I wasn't Donnell. And I had a caveman to hide before the rescue team came.

I sent the vidcam back out to look for the smilodon, but he was nowhere in sight. That gave me the time to fetch my sample bag and recover a millilitre, nearly twenty drops, of smilodon urine from the gauze pad. I put it in a vial and tucked it into my supply case. Then I checked my screen again. The meadow was empty. In the river, a giant beaver swam, then dove beneath the surface. Near the far bend, where the river widened and became shallow, a huge bear appeared. It lumbered out of the woods and stood on its hind legs, sniffing the air. Standing like that, it must have been over two metres tall. Then it dropped back down on four legs and went to the edge of the river. It wasn't a cave bear – those had already died out. But it was a huge bear nonetheless. It stood at the side of the river, seemingly lost in thought, sunning itself, then all of a sudden it launched itself into the water.

73

The water frothed and boiled, and the bear disappeared in the heaving depths as it dove to grab something. It reappeared a moment later holding a thrashing giant salmon. The bear grasped the fish's tail with its powerful jaws while it slashed at it with its front legs, its long claws ripping shreds of flesh and skin off.

The salmon was far too big for the bear to hold, and with a desperate wrench, it flung itself free. It was badly wounded but would probably survive. The bear was left with a chunk of fish tail, and it wasted no time scooping up the scraps left floating in the water. After, it stood in the river and drank, all the while keeping an eye out for another fish.

Fascinated, I watched, ignoring the glyptodon as it started to trample my tent. I didn't care. I'd sort the mess out later. I was safe behind a small perimeter with Yah, and I had some supplies with me. The day's exertions caught up to me as I prepared a report and recorded it on my comlink. I lay down and rested for just a minute. When I next opened my eyes, the sun had started to set.

Chapter Ten

I woke up to a rhythmic thumping. For a minute I didn't know where the sound came from, then I raised my head and saw Yah busy whacking his cast with a stone. The medbot had encased his leg from the waist to his ankle, so Yah could barely sit up. He lay on his side and hit the cast, an expression of grim determination on his face.

When I stood, meaning to try to explain, he threw the stone at me and rolled over, hiding his face with his hands and wailing. He was terrified. I couldn't blame him. He hadn't been aiming for me. The medbot, perhaps alerted by the sound, was trotting over, antennas raised, lights blinking, to assess the situation. I grabbed my sleeping bag that I'd left outside, and tossed it over the bot, hiding it.

'It's not dangerous. Don't be afraid. I'm sorry.' I crouched by Yah and gently took his hands. 'I'm sorry you were frightened. The medbot is harmless. I know you can't understand me, but listen to my voice. Listen, nothing will hurt you. I promise.'

He was trembling, but he lowered his hands. He pointed at his cast. '*Shika, doonidsta!*'

'I still can't understand you. I wish I had a linguist with me,' I said, patting his shoulder. 'The medbot is our friend.' I laughed suddenly. That's what kids were told in my time. I put my right hand thumb on my left hand pinkie and then switched over, making a little spider hand puppet. 'The medbot is our friend, it heals us of our woes. From the tip top of our head to the tippy of our toes.' I sang the little lullaby mothers sang to their children. Then I stopped.

I let my hands drop to my sides. *How had I known that?* The song was in my head. I could hear it. I could hear her voice. She was . . .

'Robin, *shika! Shika Yah*,' Yah begged, grabbing at me and pointing to his cast.

I shook the vague memories away. What good did it do now if I remembered or not? *Shika* must mean help, in Yah's language. I would try to help him understand. I looked around and found what I needed. A stick. I picked it up and brought it to Yah. I put the stick next to my leg, then, I bent the stick until it cracked. I pretended to be hurt, and limped, moaning. I showed Yah the broken stick and pointed to his leg. Then I took my sleeping bag off the medbot and gave the stick to the bot. It took it with one of its grippers, made a little chirp, and then straightened the stick and squirted a bright neon green cast on the break. The bot was pretty cool.

Yah had not grasped the concept. At the sight of the bot, he scrabbled on the ground, looking for another rock to throw at it.

'No, it's not a bad bot. Look!' I handed the stick with the little cast on it to Yah, who threw it at the bot. The stick broke in half, and the little bot chirped happily and fixed it, putting the two ends together and spinning a sunset-coloured cast over the break. It trotted over to me, holding the stick up, green lights blinking. I shooed the bot away and turned to Yah.

'That's enough now. You have to eat something, then sleep, and I have to think of a way to keep you safe. The rescue team should arrive soon, and I don't want them to find you. If they don't eliminate you completely, they'll bleed you dry to get your blood. I don't want to scare you, but they'll take you prisoner and treat you like an animal. I won't let that happen. Let's try and think of a way to hide you, all right?'

I deactivated my perimeter and went to check my supplies in the demolished tent. The glyptodon had gone. I kept an eye on my floating screen, set to the security cams. I sent my vidcam hovering high above. The sky was clear and calm, I had a good picture of the encampment and the surrounding area.

I'd shrunk the screen to the smallest size, so Yah wouldn't notice

76

it as much. In my supplies, I found some self-heating meals. I chose vegetarian for myself, and beef for Yah. I checked the ingredients. He'd probably get sick on anything with gluten or too many spices in it. The beef was just a basic meat and mashed potato meal. There were also carrots, and it would probably be horribly salty to his taste. I also found some dried fruit. And chocolate. I hesitated, then shrugged. It wasn't like he was going to tell anyone.

Yah was starving, but he was leery of the food. I didn't know what to serve it in. I had cornstarch plasticine plates and cutlery; everything was so biodegradable that if it rained, I'd probably lose half my belongings. I finally just put his food on a plate and set it next to him.

I sat next to him and ate, using my fingers, and he narrowed his eyes and sniffed at his dinner.

'Go on, it's good,' I said.

He propped himself up on one arm, and reached over to the food. It wasn't hot, but he wasn't expecting it to be so warm. He looked around, confused. I could tell he was searching for my fire. Then he sniffed at it again, dipped his finger in the mashed potatoes and gravy, and tasted it.

I've never seen a self-heating meal disappear so fast. He scooped it into his mouth, grinning and talking, eating, swallowing, talking, and eating some more. I have no idea what he was saying but one of the words must have meant 'Good!' because he finished everything then licked the plate, then took a bite out of the plate (technically the cornstarch plasticine was edible, but it probably tasted awful). He spat out the pieces of plate.

I finished more slowly, keeping an eye on Yah to see how his digestive system was handling the food. Now he must be thirsty, so I got my water pouches out. Water pouches have electrolytes in them, and they are easy to store – the square pouch is puncture-proof, but if you put the corner in your mouth, human saliva creates a drinking valve that you can reseal after use. I showed Yah how it worked, and he caught on quickly. He also spent a lot of time poking, prodding, and squeezing the pouch.

Now it was time for dessert. I took a small bar of chocolate and broke it in half. I gave it to him, and watched as he examined it. I took a bite, showing him how to eat it. He sniffed at it, licked it, and then closed his eyes. The first smile I'd seen from him bloomed on his face. He put the chocolate in his mouth, took it out again, drooled on it, licked it and chewed it, licked his fingers. Sighed deeply. The chocolate was gone. He lay back, his arms crossed over his chest. I tapped his arm and he looked at me and said something. His chocolate smile had faded. He looked forlorn.

'Sorry. Still *no comprendo*,' I said. I *was* sorry. I would have loved to have been able to talk to him, to ask him about his life, and to tell him about the future. I decided to build a fire, that would make him feel more relaxed, I thought. I gathered some sticks and brush and put my firestarter in it. A tongue of flame licked up, and soon a fire was crackling merrily.

Yah stared at it, and stared at me. He gabbled something, pointing to the firestarter.

'Clever, isn't it? Look, it's easy. I'll show you when you're feeling better. Now, I think I better help you to the bathroom. It's actually a latrine pit, but I think you'll get the idea.'

I helped him to his feet and half carried, half guided him to the pit I'd dug down the hill a-ways, behind a boulder. It was a long hike for him, and he was trembling with fatigue when we finally made it back. I activated both the inner and the outer safety perimeters, then put my sleeping bag on the ground and had Yah lie down on it. Then I took my washing kit and bathed him. He fell asleep before I finished.

I was exhausted too, but I had to find a way to hide him. I had no idea when the rescue team would arrive, but usually, when someone sent an alert, like I'd done, the team left within forty-eight hours.

I sent my vidcam on a recon mission, checking for animals. Then I fixed my tent, picked up my supplies, and sorted through the supplies that Donnell had had as well. After, inside my tent, I set up my lab. As I worked, an idea formed in my head. I could hide Yah in my tent. If I used Donnell's tent and put it over mine, hiding the double entrance and making it look like it was still just one tent, I could make a space for Yah in between the two tents. The tents were reshapable, so I could tweak and bend them at will.

I pitched Donnell's tent over the top of mine and lined the two entrances up. Then I pulled my tent flaps out and fastened them to the outside of Donnell's tent. From the outside, it looked like one tent. There was no way you could tell that, on the right, there was a full half-metre difference between the inside and the outside of the tent. I cut a flap in the side wall, next to my bed, and I was in between the two tents. There, I used Donnell's sleeping bag and some of his gear to fix up a small space for Yah. The tent was temp-treated – it stayed warm in cold weather, and was agreeably cool in the heat.

I called up my medbot and programmed it to take care of Yah. Sleep would be the best bet until his leg healed. I queried when that would be, and the bot flashed a reply. He would be walking in two days. The bone cement would be hard enough to support his weight and the cast would melt off. Could he safely sleep for two days? I asked the medbot.

The bot burbled and beeped, then cheeped, and listed what it would do – intravenous, catheter, electric stimuli for the muscles, monitoring. Then it bustled off to scan Yah. I got back to straightening up my gear.

A loud scream startled me, and I rushed out. Yah had woken up when the bot started probing. I managed to calm him down, and gained a major victory when Yah let the bot touch him. The bot gave him some happy juice, as I called the mild sedative, and soon Yah was relaxed enough for me to help him hobble into my tent. He wasn't happy about the lab, but when he was lying in the narrow space between the inner and outer tent walls, he calmed down. The dark reassured him, the sleeping bag was more comfortable than the pile of animal skins, and soon he nodded off.

I rubbed the sleep from my eyes and got the material the bot needed for Yah, then, when I was sure he was securely sedated for the next two days, I closed the flap I'd cut in the tent, put my bed in front of it, lay down, and soon passed out. As I drifted off to sleep, a voice sang in my head. *'The medbot is our friend, it heals us of our woes. From the tip top of our head to the tippy of our toes.'*

Chapter Eleven

I awoke during the night. Something had made a noise outside. I got out of bed, pulled on a pair of pants, and realized my cast had already disappeared. My arm felt stiff and ached, but everything seemed back in place. The noise came again. A sort of plaintive coo. The glyptodon stood just at the edge of the outer perimeter, shuffling its feet, and every now and then it stretched its head out and touched the perimeter with its nose. When that happened, a bright spark would arc into the air, startling the beast, and it would retreat.

'Hey, I'm sorry, but I can't let you in,' I said, walking towards the big creature. I deactivated a square in the inner perimeter and stepped through. I was going to the latrine pit, but before I left the safety of the outer perimeter I quickly scanned the area with my vidcam. I set it on infrared. No wolves, no smilodon. But in my tent, I noticed the faint outline of Yah. I'd have to hang a reflective liner. Hopefully I could rig something up. Otherwise I could put the brightly glowing battery pack nearer that wall – the glow would disguise his outline if anyone scanned my tent.

I picked up my shovel, deactivated a portion of my outer perimeter, and quickly hiked down to the latrine pit. That done, I went back and watched the glyptodon as it grazed as near as he could get to his 'mate'. He'd figured out where the perimeter was and had stopped testing it. For now. I made sure it was activated, then went back to bed, after dragging the battery pack to the foot of my bed.

★

'Robin! Robin Johnson!'

I rolled out of bed, still in my rumpled clothes, and staggered outside. Thick morning mist hid the valley. The sun hadn't quite risen yet, but the sky had begun to turn grey around the edges. The voice had come from the bottom of the hill. I sent my vidcam and opened my floating screen. In a minute, I was looking at four men, standing around the rock pile I'd put on top of Donnell. I clicked my comlink, and sent a message. The men looked up at the sound of my vidcam – and their faces appeared on my floating screen. I enlarged it and stared.

Four men, and obviously they had taken the time to recuperate after their voyage, although they still looked faintly stunned. I knew how they felt. I looked closer. I recognized two of the men who had been with Donnell the first time he'd come here. The time he'd infected the animals with the typhus. A third man looked familiar. There was something about him. My skin crawled – *why?* It took a minute before I placed him. *Mars.* The vid that Donnell had made. Donnell had filmed their meeting, and that's where I'd seen him before. But there was something else. Before I could dwell on it, I noticed the last man. My breath caught in my throat. *Jake!*

I heard a buzz and saw a vidcam zooming towards me. I quickly rearranged my expression and waved at the cam.

'I'm at the top of the hill. There are several boulders, you'll see my tent just behind them. I'll shut down the perimeters,' I said.

My mind was working furiously. I had to get Jake alone and find out what he knew. It didn't surprise me to see him here. He was, after all, a wild animal expert. But I had to know if he was in on the crime the others had committed. *Oh, no, not Jake*, I thought miserably. And the other men – what would they do when they realized what had happened to Donnell? I gnawed my fingernails. Did they have to know? I could tell them he had been killed by the pack of wolves. Not a trace of him left. That might buy me more time.

I kept a big grin on my face as I deactivated the perimeters and got ready to greet my rescuers. I had to make them believe I was relieved to see them and . . . I nearly gasped. *The medbot!* Every operation was recorded. I spun around and heedless of how odd it

81

may have looked, ran into my tent. The vidcam tried to follow me but I was too quick – I shut the tent flap, pounced on the medbot and pulled the drive out of its base.

'Hurry, hurry, hurry,' I breathed, pressing my comlink to the drive and erasing it. When nothing was left I shoved the drive back into the bot's base. I flipped my toilet kit open. The men were going to wonder why I'd disappeared into my tent so fast. I shoved a couple toothpaste tablets in my mouth and chomped them as I ran back outside and threw myself into Jake's arms. I pressed my mouth to his, giving him a fresh, toothpaste kiss. 'Oh, Jake! I'm such a mess,' I said, stepping back and pretending to smooth my short hair. 'I haven't slept, it's been horrible. I'm so glad you're here.' I stopped, pretended to be flustered, and greeted the other men, who were staring at me.

The tallest man stepped forward, 'Where's—'

'I can't believe you got here. I've been waiting, it's been so awful, I'm so, so glad to see you. I'm Robin,' I interrupted, stammering with what I hoped sounded like sheer relief.

The men introduced themselves. Santiago de los Réos was the man who'd met Donnell on Mars. I classified him as the business end of the operation. Tall, thin, with an expensive, tattoo comlink on the back of his hand. I didn't recognize the drawing he'd chosen. It looked like a Japanese kanji symbol. When he saw my interest, he smoothly lowered his arm, and when he next raised it, I saw the symbol had changed subtly. Again my skin prickled. Something about the man repulsed me.

Captain Hackab was an older, wiry, athletic man who'd been in charge of the first operation in the past, and he put emphasis on the word Captain, making sure I realized he was someone with authority. The third man just said his name was Brett, and he gave me what he must have thought was a boyish grin and shook my hand, holding it longer than I would have liked. I recognized him as being the one with the protective suit and the flea shaker. He brushed a lock of sandy hair out of his eyes and said, 'So you're the famous Robin Johnson. You must be surprised to see Jake. How long have you

82

been working for his father? You know, I was one of Dr Powell's first assistants before I quit to get my doctorate.'

I reset my opinion of him. One of my boss's ex-assistants – I wondered how long he'd lasted. 'Yes, I'm Robin Johnson, and I'm not surprised to see Jake. He's been chasing after me for ages. It was just a matter of time before he caught up. So, you must be a doctor. Dr Brett . . . ?' I waited for his last name, but he shook his head.

'No formalities here. Just Brett is fine.'

I took a deep breath and smiled brightly. 'Well, now we can get to work and get out of here. When is the pickup beam coming for us?'

Captain Hackab said, 'It's set to pick us up in seven days. We have one week to collect specimens and to make the films the museum ordered.'

'That's why I'm here.' Jake raised his hand. 'I'm here to help Donnell. Where is he? Still sleeping?' His voice had gone brittle, and I thought I knew why. Only one tent?

'Yes, where *is* Donnell? We got the alert, but of course no one knew who sent it or why.' Captain Hackab sounded accusing, as if I'd sent the alert on a whim.

'Donnell was killed just minutes after we got here. That's why I sent the alert. When we arrived, the, the protective bubble, the electrical barrier that was supposed to linger while we recovered from the trip, shut down sooner than Donnell expected. The wolves came out of the forest down there.' I pointed to the edge of the forest, on the far side of the meadow. 'We saw them as they came out of the forest. Instead of setting up a safety perimeter right away, Donnell decided we should head for higher ground. The wolves didn't seem to notice us at first. But before we knew it, they'd surrounded us. Donnell pushed me on top of that boulder and was going to fight the wolves off, but they – they tore him to pieces. It was awful. He was still dizzy from the voyage.'

I stopped and put my hands over my face. Then I sank to my knees and bent over. I was such a terrible actress that I was sure the men would see through my lie. But Jake knelt to comfort me, while Captain Hackab gave orders for a new safety perimeter, large enough to allow for five tents, to be built.

'Where is Donnell's gear?' asked Santiago, and I could tell he was trying to sound casual.

'The wolves ate most of him, then a bear chased the wolves off and dragged his torso away. His backpack was still attached to it. And an *Argentavis magnificens*, a vulture,' I added, seeing his blank look, 'came and took what was left. It gulped down Donnell's head, his boots, and another one of his backpacks that was covered with blood. It even ate the bones that the bear left.' I stopped and gagged. I was telling a gruesome tale. I couldn't just talk. I had to react. I clapped my hands over my mouth, as if I was about to vomit, and rushed into my tent.

'Robin, wait,' said Jake, and he followed me.

I pretended to retch and grabbed a Mylar bag. I turned towards Jake but kept my eyes lowered. I didn't want to meet his eyes. I didn't want to know he'd been a part of wanting to spread a deadly disease in the past and present – for whatever reason. I couldn't bear to know he had been a part of the plan to kill me. A plan that had backfired spectacularly.

A thought occurred to me. Who else knew about the pellet? Who had tampered with it? Was one of the men out there wondering why I hadn't dissolved into a pile of pink jelly? Or Jake? Suddenly my sickness wasn't feigned. I barely had time to open the Mylar bag before I threw up in it.

Jake was at my side, holding my shoulders. The tent flap lifted, and Brett came in. He watched me retching, and frowned. 'This campsite will do. We're setting up. Jake, where do you want your tent?'

Jake's hands tightened on my shoulders. 'I'm going to stay with Robin. She shouldn't be alone after such a shock. And my father will kill me if I don't bring her back in one piece,' he joked.

I didn't dare look at him, instead I concentrated on what I had to do. Get the samples. Find out if any of these men meant to kill me. Keep Yah out of sight until I could find a way to get him to his cave and hidden.

'We're going on a reconnaissance hike in two hours. Be ready,' said Brett – speaking to Jake. He ducked out of the tent. I glanced after him and froze. One of the flaps had come undone, and the double tent was visible from the inside.

'I want you to look at my lab,' I said to Jake, pointing to the back of the tent. 'Make sure I have everything, will you?' When he swung around to look, I went to the doorway and fixed the flap. Outside, Brett had yet to start pitching his tent. He tapped something on his comlink, a floating screen hovering in front of him. Captain Hackab had an arsenal of weapons on the ground and studied them intently, as if trying to decide which ones to take with him. Santiago was nowhere to be seen, but his tent was set up. It was closest to the boulder, and I thought that was a strange place to set up a tent. The smilodon could easily leap from the rock to the tent. But then I saw the perimeter had been enlarged to encompass the boulder as well. The men were taking no chances.

The morning mist burned away. The men took over, making a schedule, giving orders (to me, mostly), treating me like a secretary, making sure I had the lab set up correctly and was ready to take notes. I played the meek woman who'd been through a traumatic experience and needed strong, competent men around to take over. The men were itching to go exploring, so, when the sun reached the noon zenith, they set off. I stayed behind, keeping in my meek role.

While they hiked down the hill, I sent my vidcam after them, to keep an eye on them. They paused to look at the pile of stones I'd set up for Donnell, and my comlink crackled.

'What's this?' asked Captain Hackab.

'What's what?' I didn't want him to know I was watching them on a screen.

'This pile of stones halfway down the hill.'

'Oh. I put it there to remind me where the tractor beam will be for the return trip. I didn't want to miss it.' A thought occurred to me. 'Why are we staying two extra days? I was supposed to go back after only a week. Now it will be nine days. I have to admit, I'm nervous about cutting it so close with that *ta me da* pellet in my butt. I don't feel like melting.'

Captain Hackab just shrugged. 'Don't worry. Make sure you have the specimen bags ready. And we'll bring dinner. Don't worry.'

I looked at my comlink. Captain Hackab was itching to kill something and grill it. I wondered briefly what he'd have thought of Yah's gruesome dinner. I shuddered and got to work. First things first. I scanned the area for cams. I didn't want anyone to see what I was about to do. *Ah.* A vidcam lurked just on top of the boulder by Santiago's tent. I watched it out of the corner of my eye, and just as I thought – it followed me as I moved around the campsite. I pretended to be checking the perimeter, then I went inside my tent.

I sat on my bed and fumed. Santiago de los Réos, whoever he was, the fucker, was watching me. I cut a slit in the back of my tent. From there, I sent my vidcam out. I opened a floating screen and scanned my campsite. There was only one camera monitoring me. But were there others in the tents? Avoiding the line of sight of the cam on the rock was easy – it was aimed at my tent. I swooped my vidcam into Captain Hackab's tent. No cams. No traps. Just weapons galore. I looked for any sort of computer – a comlink, a vidcam. He must have everything with him. His camping gear looked worn but high-quality. I sent the vidcam in closer. Very high-quality, and worth a fortune. I looked up the brand of his tent. It cost as much as six months of my salary. His gear came from an exclusive manufacturer that specialized in made-to-order items. I looked up Captain Hackab and my comlink said that he worked freelance, and often accompanied Tempus U's scientists on dangerous trips to the past. His specialty was survival in some of the most dangerous circumstances. He wasn't a specialist in large animals – that was Jake. Captain Hackab was a survival expert and well known in his profession. He was also very wealthy, if his equipment was anything to go by.

I sent my vidcam into Santiago's tent. No lab. No sample bags. No weapons. Why was he here? Who was he? He'd met Donnell on Mars, that was for sure. He must work for Tempus U, but in what capacity? And why did he seem so familiar to me? He must be about my age, maybe a few years older. I searched my memory but came up with nothing.

Two large backpacks rested on the floor of the tent near the foot of his bed. I couldn't see what they held. I swivelled the vidcam around, searching for clues. I didn't want to get caught, so I sent the vidcam outside, checked that the cam spying on me was still in the same place, and strolled out of my tent and looked around. I thought a good thing to do would be to act as if I were afraid to leave the perimeter, so I called up a floating screen and sat in the doorway of my tent, pretending to write notes. After a while, I went back into my tent and checked on Yah. Still asleep. Looking peaceful. I closed the panel and went to my lab and started analyzing the samples I'd already collected from the dire wolves. There wasn't much to discover. One of the animals had mange. The blood tested positive for the Typhus-77 antibodies. It matched the profile of the virus back in my time. That didn't surprise me. I'd already realized that the virus had been man-made and that Donnell and his accomplices had spread it here over a hundred years ago, thanks to the time-travel program.

I needed to know who had sanctioned that trip – because there was no way a trip could have been done clandestinely. On a hunch, I looked up Santiago's profile. I shook my head. I was such a *bèn đàn!* *How* could I have missed that? Because of his last name, I hadn't made the connection. Santiago de los Réos was one of the scions of the Carlysle Corporation. His mother had been a Carlysle – part of the group which financed in part the time travel institute, as well as being the main shareholders in the Mars Corporation, the conglomerate that ruled Mars. If Santiago wanted to go back in time, he could literally go back as a tourist. He could bring friends with him. He'd already done so on occasion – and each time, the trip was done as a private jaunt. He didn't make films, he didn't do research – he didn't have to. His family was one of the wealthiest on Mars, and that was saying something. As far as I knew, he didn't hold a job in Tempus U. He was listed on the board of directors, but there were hundreds of people on the board. Including Dr Powell. I must have seen him on a news holo, although he was reputed to be very discreet.

Think, Robin – *think*. Why is he here *now*? Why had he met Donnell on Mars? I nearly slapped myself. I kept thinking like someone with some sort of moral compass. He had none. He was with Donnell because he had financed the virus. I put it all together now. Santiago had paid for the virus to be developed. Brett had been the scientist. Donnell had been hired to accompany them as a wild animal specialist, and Captain Hackab had been with them for protection. Santiago had made sure the trip remained – while not completely a secret – at least out of Tempus U's program. He must have paid for the whole thing himself, meaning to recoup the cost with the antibodies and the vaccine when he got back to our time. Even if the time-travel had cost him a billion Mars credits, which would be about a hundred million Western State of California dollars, he'd still be assured of making a thousand times more by selling the vaccine in the future.

In the future, where millions of people were panicking because a lethal virus had appeared. A virus that Santiago had paid for, that Brett had developed, and that Donnell and Captain Hackab knew about, and probably had invested in. And Jake in all this? *Please let him be innocent*, I muttered, as I finished writing down everything I'd discovered and encrypting it. Then I sat back and started planning. I had one day to find out what Jake knew, two days to think of a plan for getting Yah back to his cave and hidden, and one week to help find a vaccine that would save millions.

PART II

Cruelty has a Human heart
And Jealousy a Human Face,
Terror, the Human Form Divine,
And Secrecy, the Human Dress.

From 'A Divine Image' by William Blake (1757-1827)

Chapter Twelve

Because they'd hiked all afternoon and were still suffering from time-travel sickness, because of the safety perimeter, because of the vidcams, and lulled by a safe sense of technology, the men in the camp were not as attentive as they could have been.

Yah woke sometime in the middle of the night. I heard him stir, and I crept in between the tent walls to see him. So as not to startle him, I had the medbot give him a nice dose of happy juice. The cast was starting to dissolve. As I watched, it shrivelled and turned to a fine dust. Yah had healed much faster than the medbot had predicted, but it didn't surprise me. His organism had never had antibiotics, vitamins, or modern medicine, and everything had worked with stunning efficiency and swiftness. *And speaking of modern medicine.*

My medbot is my friend, I hummed, as I programmed the little bot. I sent it scurrying away to Jake's bed. It delicately probed Jake's hand, which hung over the side of the bed, and gave him a tiny injection. He'd sleep soundly for hours.

The bot did a little jig and chirped softly. I programmed it for silence and sent it off to the other three men's tents; everyone would sleep tonight. I sent my vidcam out and found the cams that had been placed for security, and then I took Yah's hand and we slipped out of the tent, keeping out of sight of Santiago's spycams. This was easy. Yasmine and I had often snuck past spycams at the university or out of her parents' house to go partying. And in case one of the cams had been programmed to check on me later, I simply filmed myself lying down, projected my image on to a floating screen hovering just above my bed, and put it on a loop. It took less than a minute.

Light from the full moon silvered the grass in the meadow and cast mysterious shadows beneath the trees. Stars glittered in the heavens. The Milky Way stretched like a river of diamond dust across the sky. A nightbird called from somewhere in the forest, and from far away, came an answering hoot.

Yah was high on happy juice, and pointed at everything, then caught sight of his own hand and stopped to wonder at it. I tugged his arm and made him hurry, I was worried about the wolves, but they were nowhere to be seen. No glyptodon either. No smilodon. I kept my floating screen right by me, and Yah kept poking holes in it with his fingers and laughing.

Humans high on drugs all act basically the same. Big stupid grin, slurry words, uncontrollable laughter. Yah thought my floating screen was hilarious. I kept trying to make him be quiet, but finally gave up and just concentrated on keeping him hurrying along.

After an hour or so, the drugs started to wear off. He stopped grinning and started to look worried. He turned to me and made signs with his hands – he was trying to tell me something but I had no idea what it could be. We made a halt, and I took food out of my backpack and gave him some dried fruit and a water pouch. He gobbled the fruit and drained the water pouch. I gave him another one. He put it on his head and started giggling again.

I got him to his feet and he looked around. Then he tugged on my arm and made the signs again. I suddenly got it.

'I left your spear in my tent. *Merde, merde, merde!*' I swore.

'*Merde*,' agreed Yah. He had a pretty good French accent for a Palaeolithic guy.

'I'm sorry. I left it hidden in my tent. I'll get it back to you. I promise. Now, we have to get *you* hidden. I know you want to go back to your cave, but the best thing would be for you to leave this area until we're gone.' I checked my floating screen and sighed. 'You have no idea what I'm saying, but at least you're not in the campsite.

I'll try to keep the others away from you. You must stay away from them.' I pointed in the direction of my campsite and gave a low whistle. I was trying to tell him it was dangerous there.

He grunted and poked at my floating screen some more. He looked at his fingers, then poked the screen again.

'Hurry. I have to be back before daybreak and before the others wake up. They are going to have splitting headaches, but they will think it was from time travel,' I added. That didn't bother me. What bothered me was Yah. His cave would be discovered, along with the bodies of his family. And if they did find Yah and realize he'd survived the epidemic, they'd kill him for his blood.

Well, unless I killed them first. They were asleep. I could cut their throats. No, that would mean I'd go to prison. Not an option. I'd been in an asylum for the insane, if anything happened, I'd be right back there, and this time there'd be no getting out. I couldn't programme the medbot to kill – they simply could not kill anyone on purpose. I would have to think of some other solution.

After what seemed like a long time, we arrived at the foot of the cliff. Yah seemed to understand that I had to leave him there. He wasn't happy and kept pointing to his cave. I was about to turn to leave, when he said, 'Ronin.'

'Robin,' I corrected gently.

'Robin.' He put his hand on my shoulder. 'Azeez aho Yah. Mesha, Na, Ebna Yahmi. Robin Yahmi' He said something else, but I'd gotten the gist. His family. Mesha, his wife, Na and Ebna, his children. And me.

I tilted my face to the stars. I understood what he wanted. And so I followed him to his cave, and I helped him push and pull the funeral pyre to the hearth in the middle of the cave, and I used my firestarter on it. We watched them burn. The tar, or whatever the bodies had been soaked in, burned quickly. Yah chanted something as they burned. I stood, silent, trying to stay out of the smoke. Then, while the flames were still bright, I climbed down the cliff and washed the smoke off in the river. I waved to Yah, standing at the mouth of his cave. He hesitated, then gave a hesitant wave.

I left, and didn't look back. I'd find a way to get his spear back to him. But before that, I had to protect him. Question was, how?

My hike back to the camp went without a problem. My vidcam and floating screen showed all clear. Not a creature was stirring, except an owl, skimming over the meadow, hunting for mice. Back in my tent, I erased all traces of Yah and hid his spear between my bed and the tent wall. I checked the men – still sleeping soundly. The drugs had worn off, now they were simply asleep. I was careful not to make any noise. Last, I turned off my floating screen and slid under my covers.

Exhaustion made my eyelids burn, and I shivered with fatigue. I checked my comlink. The sun would rise in an hour. The medbot *was* my friend. I needed to sleep then to wake up refreshed. It concocted a mixture of injections – one for instant sleep, another set to wake me up, and still another to keep me awake and alert the next day. I'd pay for it later. Much later, I hoped.

I barely made it to my bed before the first shot kicked in and I dropped into the arms of Morpheus.

When I woke up, I was disoriented for a minute. By the warm light of the overhead glow-globe, I saw that Jake wasn't in his cot. The tent flap was open. I looked out and saw smoke from a campfire rising into the still dark air. The men had reverted to their more primitive side. They greeted me with a thermos of hot maté, which they had been sharing. I poured myself a cup, and raised it in a toast.

'To my rescuers,' I said.

Jake looked pleased. 'Is that what I am?'

I yawned. The sun had yet to rise and stars still lit the night sky, but the horizon has started to turn pink at the edges. I sat on a log facing the river and sipped my hot maté.

Daybreak in the dawn of the Holocene era. The sun rose over the river, so the giant spruce forest on the far side was lit first. The tips of the trees turned silver, then gold. Then the light filtered between the branches and sparkled on the river's brown water. Huge clumps of sedge grass dominated the marshland near the river, and then came the meadow, and what I thought of as the wolves' forest beyond.

Captain Hackab called up a floating screen and turned it so we could all see. It seemed to be a detailed schedule. He stood and pointed to the first line. 'Today, Jake, you will take Santiago to the spruce forest on the other side of the river and look for mammoths. We need as much footage as possible of them. I will go with Robin to the forest where we were yesterday to finish scouting for the pack of wolves she saw. Brett, since you sprained your ankle yesterday, you can take over Robin's work today.'

Sprained his ankle? I hadn't noticed. But now I saw he walked with a slight limp.

'We'll set off in an hour. Be ready,' said Captain Hackab to me. 'Bring your sample kit.'

As if I'd forget.

I packed my sample kit, some water pouches, and some extra Mylar bags just in case. The day promised to be scorching, with not a cloud in sight. I was glad we'd be in the woods, and we'd be away from the camp. The further we were from Yah, the better it would be. Brett, with his sprained ankle, would stay close to the tents. From the other side of the river, the cave would be visible but only from a certain angle. Jake and Santiago were going to cross the river at the widest, shallowest part and enter the forest where the marsh sloped into the meadowland. They wouldn't be able to see the cave from where they were headed. I hoped that the smoke from the funeral pyre wouldn't be visible either. I thought not. I hadn't seen it from up on the bluff, and by now, the fire should be well out. Yah would be safe for today.

Captain Hackab walked quickly. He carried at least three weapons with him, and he wore a knife strapped to his leg. We hiked down the hill, crossed the meadow, and entered the forest as the sun rose above the treetops. Birds had started singing, and dew sparkled on the grass and leaves. I wondered where the glyptodon was, and hoped I'd see him soon.

We entered the forest and the light dimmed as branches criss-crossed above us. 'Where are we headed?' I asked. I'd left my vidcam back at the base camp. Taking a page from Santiago's spy book, I'd hidden it, and set it to watch my belongings. I still had to find out who, if anyone, knew Donnell had tried to kill me.

'Yesterday we found where we think the wolves built a lair. We won't get too close, but we'll try to find some samples for you. What I'd like to do is shoot one so you can get blood.'

'Do you mean shoot to kill?' That wasn't how we usually got samples.

'No, I'll tranquillize it. Don't worry.' He had a floating screen map in front of him to guide us. His vidcam was set to hover about fifty metres above us, and I noticed he'd neglected to put the infra-red cam on. On the screen, he was represented as a glowing orange dot. I wasn't on the screen at all, so I asked him why. 'Because I have a special implant that can help localize me. If the wind picks up and the vidcam is useless, I need my partners at the base camp to know where I am.'

That made sense. Vidcams were great – until the wind got too strong. Then, being light and not particularly strong flyers, they couldn't be used. But if someone had an implant, then a partner could follow their movements and track them. Floating screens were also useless in high wind, and in the forest they weren't very practical. Every branch and leaf shredded the image, and soon Captain Hackab shut down his screen and pulled out an antique handheld one.

'I haven't seen one of those in a while,' I said.

He just grunted and ducked under a branch. 'The land starts going uphill for a while, and we'll reach the ridge in about two hours. Then we head downhill. The wolves have made their home in that valley. It's deep, and on the far side are several caves.'

I hitched my backpack higher on my hips and wished I'd gotten more sleep the night before. My bones felt tired, and I thought that if I closed my eyes, I'd fall asleep while walking.

To take my mind off my fatigue I tried to get Captain Hackab to talk but he only answered in monosyllables or grunts, then he turned and snapped, 'You have to be quiet. If the wolves are around, you'll scare them off. From now on, until I say – we don't speak. Is that clear?'

I nodded, and pulled a water pouch from my pocket and drank some. I remembered Yah putting it on his head and clowning around, and that made me grin. We reached the top of the ridge after two hours and sat down to rest. Still no talking. I didn't mind. Captain Hackab opened his floating screen again and checked the area. I looked over his shoulder at the screen but didn't see anything except treetops. The view from the vidcam was limited to the area just around us. I didn't feel worried. After all, I was sitting next to a heavily armed survival expert. If anything attacked us, he'd easily fight it off. I took a meal pack from my pocket and ate some tasteless mush, then sealed the pack and put it away.

The sun had climbed along with us and now hung nearly over-head. The heat was making my head spin. The only thing I wanted to do was lie down and nap, but Hackab motioned at me to approach and then held his hand out to halt me. I stopped and cocked my head to listen, but didn't hear anything. 'What is it?' I whispered.

He'd enlarged his floating screen and was peering at it. 'I think I see something moving in the valley. It's not a dire wolf. Come over here and take a look. Tell me what you see.'

I hoped it was the smilodon. I wanted to get another glimpse of it. At the moment, I didn't think it odd that someone with a floating screen that incorporated binocular vision should ask my opinion. I climbed onto the rock next to him and looked down at the screen. Before I could spot anything, he gave me a mighty shove and I flew off the cliff.

Luckily, Captain Hackab was more proficient in survival than murder. I still had my backpack on, and it broke my fall. So instead of my back fracturing on the rocks, my backpack split open and caught on a point of one of them. I hung for a second, and for that second I thought maybe I was saved. Then everything snapped off – rock and backpack frame, and I dropped into the dense brush at the base of the cliff. I landed on my right foot and didn't try to stay upright. Instead I collapsed sideways, putting my arms over my head and rolling down the steep grade, crashing through brush and branches. I had time to hope that no branch would stab me when I

97

came to another drop and fell about two metres into a fast-moving stream.

I hit the round-pebbled stream bed, but the water had broken my fall enough so that the rocks didn't break my bones. Hitting the bottom still stunned me. I couldn't move, I just let the water drag me downstream. It took all my strength to keep my face above the surface. The sun dazzled me. I gasped for breath and fought to stay conscious. The cold water helped. It numbed my hurts and cushioned me at the same time. Carefully, I started moving my arms and legs and found, to my immense relief, nothing seemed broken. The stream rounded a bend and I washed ashore on a pebble beach with large, round pebbles everywhere, polished smooth, and warm in the sun. I rolled over to lie on my stomach and breathed slowly, thinking about what had just happened.

Captain Hackab had tried to kill me. That much was clear. Now, I had to hide from him, or better, make him think he'd succeeded in killing me. He would use his vidcam to search for me. If he had infrared on his vidcam hiding in the brush wouldn't help, my body heat would give me away. If I stayed in the cold stream, I'd be hidden for a while, but it was too shallow to hide me for long. Unless I could find an overhanging tree and stay in the water and hide under that, I'd be visible from above. I pushed myself back into the water and half swam, half waded downstream and to the far side of the stream, where a dead tree lay half in, half out of the water. I barely had time to duck under a fork in the branches, when I spotted a glint in the sky. The vidcam was in the valley, scanning the area, looking for me. It would follow the trail of pieces of my backpack, the broken brush, and find the stream soon enough.

My mind raced. Survival had always been my strong point. I did my best thinking when I was sure I was about to die. I still had my comlink. First I sent an SOS to Jake, with no details. I had no time. Just *SOS. Help.* He was on the other side of the river, the other side of the camp, about four hours away, but if I could just stay alive for that long, maybe he'd find me.

Then I called up my floating screen and enabled my camera apps

98

on my comlink. I lay on my stomach in the water and got a picture of me, seen from above. I set it on my floating screen, enlarged it to life-sized, and sent it to hover on the water, near the far shore. From above, it would look like I was floating facedown. Hopefully, Hackab would think I was dead, washed up on that pebbly beach. I huddled under the massive tree trunk and kept an eye on my floating screen. It moved gently with the current, looking even more lifelike. Or rather, hopefully, more like a dead body floating in a stream.

I caught another flash of light on Hackab's vidcam and then heard the telltale deep buzz as it came in for a closer look and hovered above my floating screen. The image would hold up if viewed from the top. If he lowered the cam to water level, the subterfuge would be discovered right away; the floating screen was just a blurry grey line viewed from the side.

The cam circled around my body for a good five minutes, while I kept my breathing soft and crouched in the water beneath the fallen tree. I was downstream and only about twenty metres away, so if the vidcam only turned around and scanned the far side of the stream, I would probably be visible. But it stayed close to my 'body' until I heard branches cracking, and I realized Hackab was heading down to the stream. He'd want to pull my body out of the water and make sure I was dead.

'*Merde*,' I whispered. I waited until I caught sight of him, then I shifted my floating screen off the beach, making my 'body' swirl around and get caught in the current, then head downstream. To make the image more realistic, I sank it slightly underwater. The vidcam followed it closely, and Hackab changed course. I floated my 'body' slowly towards the middle of the river and waited in the shadows. Now that he thought he could see me, he sent the vidcam to survey the forest – which was prudent, knowing that a pack of hungry wolves roamed nearby.

I didn't think he'd take his eyes off my fake corpse, especially if I made it sink slightly and move, as if the current was grabbing it again. He splashed into the stream and waded across, the water getting deeper as he approached me. I slid more fully underwater and behind the tree. In the dappled shade, in the murky water, it would be hard to see me. He was hip-deep now, and hesitated. I saw him call up his floating screen and look at it, then glance up towards the ridge behind me. I couldn't see what he did, but I thought it might be an animal. I hoped not. I was not feeling well enough to run, just floating in the water was hard enough.

My fingers dug into the soft wood as he got nearer. Any minute now he'd discover my subterfuge and I'd be lost. My plan consisted of trying to hide for as long as possible and wait for help. I got ready to send my floating screen downstream, hoping that he'd go after it. But I had to wait until he was in deeper water, so he wouldn't have the chance to grab at it and ruin the illusion. It was harrowing trying to keep the floating screen just out of his grasp, far enough away so he couldn't see it was an illusion, but close enough to lead him on.

A ripple coming towards me caught my eye. The water curled and frothed as something large approached rapidly. What could that be? I took a deep breath and slid underwater and looked upstream, trying to see something, but the water around me was too full of silt. I heard splashing as Captain Hackab came closer. I peeked, and saw him peering at my floating screen, a frown on his face. He lifted his gun and sighted down the barrel at it, and the river seemed to explode.

I ducked and gasped – never a good idea underwater. Desperate to remain hidden, I nearly drowned myself trying not to choke. The whole tree lurched, I grabbed a branch, and then a huge wave washed over me. Sputtering, still trying to drag air into my lungs, I came to the surface and saw Captain Hackab fighting with a giant beaver in the middle of the stream. The beaver must have blundered into him, very much like I'd bumped into the one that had broken my shoulder. The beaver, standing nearly as high as Hackab's shoulders, swung its muscular tail and caught Hackab on the thigh. I heard a crack, and he collapsed, screaming. Cursing, Hackab pulled his gun out and aimed at the giant beast.

'No!' I screamed, and jumped out of my hiding place, waving my arms. The second I did that, I realized it was a bad idea, and I quickly ducked behind the fallen tree again.

Shocked by my sudden appearance, Captain Hackab missed his shot, and the beaver attacked him again, thrashing its tail and whipping the water into a white froth. This time he hit Hackab on the shoulder and the man went down, but he wasn't beaten. He fired again, and the beaver flinched. The shot must have touched it somewhere, because it plunged into the water and swam rapidly downstream.

Hackab looked around. 'Robin? Robin. Was that you? Where are you?' He must have been in terrible pain, but he kept his voice level. I saw how his skin had turned grey though, and how his hand trembled as it held the gun.

I wasn't about to show myself. I moved further behind the tree and looked at him through a tangle of dead branches. He managed to get to the shore, but could not stand. Carefully, he dragged himself onto the pebbled beach and lay there, breathing hard. I thought his left thigh, and most likely his left arm, were broken. He rolled over and tried to sit up. Cursing, he gave up, and lay there. He didn't let go of his gun, and I didn't dare approach.

He opened a floating screen and spoke into his comlink. 'Brett,' he said, his voice hoarse. 'Are you there? We have a problem. I think she got away. I'm not sure. She's probably wounded and won't get far. And I'm injured. Scan my position and send help.'

He swore, and lay back, resting the gun on his stomach.

The cold from the stream made me shiver, but I stayed put. So, Brett knew about Captain Hackab's attempt to murder me. They were in it together. That left Jake and Santiago. Santiago, I knew, was in on developing the virus. But was he a murderer as well? He made my skin crawl, but that was not proof. I needed proof before I could accuse him of trying to kill me. I had a hard time believing Jake was in on anything. Which meant he could be in danger as well. How could I warn him? Had he gotten my call for help?

I dithered, not sure what to do, as I watched Hackab. He seemed to be recovering. He managed to get up and, dragging his leg, limped off the beach. Suddenly the bushes rustled in front of him. A grey form surged out. A dire wolf. Without hesitating, it leaped on

101

Hackab and seized him by the neck. It was over in seconds. Hackab never had the chance to shoot, although he held his gun in his hand. He barely had time to yell, to scream – before the pack of wolves was upon him and devoured him. Clothing ripped as the wolves tugged and pulled, tearing cloth and scattering weapons. While they were snarling and fighting over the pieces, I let go of the tree and quietly floated downstream.

I wanted to put as much distance between me and the wolves as possible, but I was wary of meeting the beaver. However, I needn't have worried. As I rounded the bend I saw it, lying on the bank. Hackab's shot had killed the poor beast. In one way, I was relieved. If the wolves came after me, they'd probably be more interested in the already dead prey.

I let the current carry me. My head ached, my teeth chattered with cold, and I had no idea where I was. I thought that perhaps this branch of the stream must meet the river, but it would be down-stream from my campsite. I called up my floating screen and put the map of the area on it. But I didn't have my vidcam, so I couldn't locate my position. I hoped I'd be able to make an educated guess though. The problem was that there were many streams meandering through the lowlands. If I'd been on the other side of the river, it would have been easier because there was only one tributary that ran through the forest and came out not far from where I'd seen the bear fishing for salmon. But this side of the river consisted of a series of narrow, deep valleys, each with its own stream. From high above, the terrain looked like a giant eight-fingered hand, with the streams as fingers reaching out and twisting this way and that. All the streams did lead to the river, after a fashion. I thought perhaps I was in the very first stream on the map. It would actually come out not far from the base of the cliff where Yah's cave was. I was cold though. I had to get out and get warmed up.

Could I build a fire? I didn't have my firestarter kit, and I had no idea how to proceed without one. The edges of the forest came right down to the stream with trees leaning over. The forest looked dense, and I didn't like the idea of making noise, which I would do if I blundered through the bushes. The map showed the forest giving away to marsh and meadowland, both covered with huge clumps of sedge grass. I stayed in the stream, letting the current carry me. After a while, the stream I was in widened even more, and soon only a narrow channel in the middle had any current. The trees tapered off, and suddenly I was in full sunshine. Even the water warmed up as it grew shallower. A new worry was the marsh. Now, instead of rounded pebbles, there was mud. And the huge clumps of sedge grass blocked my view of anything. I stayed where the current was, although it grew fainter. Soon it was barely there, but it drew ribbons in the silt at the bottom, so I continued on. The stream grew so shallow I could touch bottom with my hands as I swam. I didn't want to stand and walk in the mud, but now I had no choice. I was ready to leave the stream entirely when I caught sight of the high bluff in the distance, far to my right. I stood shakily and held my arm into the air to take a laser reading with my comlink. Less than four kilometres away.

The problem was, the stream seemed to curve left. But at least I had a landmark now. I was about to set off again when my comlink sparked. I switched my floating screen to incoming calls. It was Jake. I nearly hugged the image on the screen from sheer relief.

'Where are you?' he asked. I could see him, so he had his vidcam with him. He couldn't see me though. I could have filmed myself with my comlink and uploaded it to my vidcam, but it seemed too much effort, all of a sudden. I tapped my comlink to retrieve my vidcam from my tent.

'I'm three point six kilometres from the base camp, by laser beam sight reckoning. Did you get my message?'

He shook his head. 'No. What message? Santiago and I just found a mammoth trail, and we're marking it so we can follow it tomorrow. I think we're going to get some great footage.'

'I sent you a message over two hours ago,' I said. 'Check your comlink again.'

He frowned at his wrist, then shook his head. 'No message from you. Where is Captain Hackab? I can't raise him either. Santiago is getting nervous. He wanted to recon with Hackab about an hour ago.'

I caught sight of Santiago, standing near Jake. He could hear me. I needed to buy time. 'I don't know where he is. We were on top of the ridge, when I stupidly tripped and fell over. Captain Hackab grabbed me – I remember that much – and then I was falling. I woke up in the water, floating downstream. I kept hoping Captain Hackab would find me – I waited to see his vidcam, but I didn't see anything. I just kept floating downstream.' I didn't need to invent a trembling voice. The cold had seeped into my bones, and the shock and stress of the past few hours was making me light-headed. 'I can see the bluff from here, but I'm injured. I don't think I can walk.'

'Don't move. I'm sending my vidcam—'

'No! Don't! I need to see you, Jake. Don't leave me. I'll be OK if I can see you. Just keep talking to me. I'll crawl out of the stream and hide in the sedge grass. You'll find me. I'll call my vidcam to me.'

'Where *is* your vidcam?'

I couldn't tell him I'd left it in my tent to spy for me, so I lied. 'Captain Hackab told me to leave it at the base camp. He had his, and it was better. He told me that mine made too much noise.' I could say whatever I wanted – Hackab wasn't going to argue with me.

Jake made a face. 'Hurry up and get your vidcam. I'm on my way to you right now. Santiago will trace Captain Hackab. He's probably looking for you. Maybe the valley is too deep and the signal isn't getting through.'

I thought of my horrific fall. 'It *was* a deep valley. And the cliff sides have copper deposits. That would block the calls. That's why you didn't get mine.' I rubbed my face. One side felt numb and swollen. I might have a broken cheekbone, I thought dispassionately. I was too tired to care about much. But I was glad Jake was on his way. I had an answer to why my call hadn't been received. And hopefully Santiago would be searching for Captain Hackab long enough for me to do something about Brett.

Chapter Thirteen

I sent for my vidcam and it came, zooming and buzzing above the tall sedge grass like a glittering hornet. When I caught sight of it, I connected it to my floating screen and programmed it to scan the area in case any predators came near. Then it was just a matter of waiting until Jake came. I found a particularly large clump of the grass and made myself a sort of nest.

The events of the day caught up with me and I couldn't stop shaking. I'd lost everything: my backpack with my supplies, my samples kit, both my boots, my pants had been torn off me, my jacket as well. All I had left were my underwear and my undershirt, and both were worse for wear. Insects tormented me, so I rolled in the mud and then crawled back to my nest, curled in a ball, and tried to rest.

'Yasmine,' I sighed, when my heart stopped thudding. 'I wish you could see me now. You'd make some sort of joke about bog monsters coming to eat me. Or that I looked like one, covered in all this mud. That's why I haven't sent my floating screen to Jake. He'd take one look and run away. Anyhow, I just wanted to tell you that I miss you. That I'll always miss you. It was really shitty of you to go and die on me like that. I mean, seriously. It's not like I have a ton of friends.'

I wasn't prepared for the grass parting, and Yah's grinning face staring down at me.

'Don't do that again! You scared me! How did you find me?'

He didn't answer but pointed to my vidcam, circling lazily above our heads. Of course. He heard it and followed it. Now he poked at my floating screen again. It was better than any toy. He also made a gesture which I recognized as being, *'Hey, where's my spear?'*

I pointed to the bluff and mimed throwing the spear. 'I'll get it back to you.' I pointed to him. My mind wasn't on the spear though. I had to get him out of here before Jake spotted him. I turned my vidcam so it looked over the marsh back towards the bluff, and kept an eye on my screen for Jake.

'I'm hurt,' I said, knowing he wouldn't understand me, but it was reassuring to be able to talk to someone. However, he had seen my face and noted my pallor. He frowned, and gently prodded my cheek. I hissed in pain and batted his hand away.

'*Shissi*,' he said, drawing back. I guessed that meant sorry. He studied me, took my arm and moved it, then motioned for me to stand up, so he could check my legs and back. 'Yah *shaki* Robin,' he said, and tugged on my hand. He meant to help lead me out of the swamp. I admit, I was tempted. The insects were swarming, and although I had smeared mud on my legs and arms, they gleefully landed on me and bit wherever there was the smallest centimetre of bare skin. Yah too had smeared his body with mud. We looked like clay creatures from a horror vid. I grinned, but motioned him away.

'Yah, you have to go now. I will be fine. Someone is coming to help me.' I looked at my floating screen, and sure enough, Jake was wading through the swamp towards me. He'd soon be near enough that I could shout. I pointed to the screen and Yah peered at it, squinting mightily, trying to understand. He looked around, then back at the screen and poked at it again.

I knew it was useless to explain. Instead I pushed him again, and pointed towards the river, making motions of shooing him away. Then I pointed again at the floating screen. I don't know what he understood, but he looked hurt. If only I could speak his language. It frustrated me, but he had to go.

Faintly, in the distance, I heard Jake call me. 'Robin! Where are you? Send me your screen!'

Yah cocked his head, listening, then suddenly he disappeared.

106

One moment he stood in front of me, the next he'd faded into the sedge grass without so much as a whisper.

I looked at the ground and saw Yah's footprints. Quickly, I rubbed them out of the mud, then I headed towards Jake, sending my floating screen on ahead so we'd meet, despite the tall grass that waved gently in the breeze and towered over our heads.

Jake found me and helped me back to the base camp. I was in no shape to confront Brett. I wasn't sure what to do about him. What I could do was get my medbot to treat me, rest, and make sure Jake was with me at all times.

Brett accosted me as soon as I set foot inside the safety perimeter, but I'd had time to think.

'What happened? Where is Captain Hackab?' Brett looked worried, and well he might – I knew he'd been in on the plan to kill me.

'I fell. It was so sudden. My foot slipped, I think. I don't remember. I fell, and then I was in the water, and I kept calling. I think I heard Hackab answer me. It gave me hope,' I said ingeniously.

'How did you get back here?'

'Leave her alone for now, Brett. Come on, Robin. Let me get you hooked up to your vitapak and medbot. You'll feel better in the morning.'

'I want to get this crust of mud off me. What do you have? Can we use some of the water packs, and a towel? Please?' I was desperate. Every part of me ached and itched.

Jake fetched three water packs and grabbed a towel, and we carefully washed off most of the muck. When that was done, I was amazed at all the bruises and cuts I had. I was black and blue and bloody all over. There were even leeches on me. 'Not another one,' I complained, as the medbot zapped a leech and it fell off me, writhing. 'That was a huge one. I wonder how much blood I lost.'

'From the looks of you, a lot,' said Jake, picking them up and putting them in a sample bag. 'You're also completely dehydrated. How much equipment did you lose?'

'All my hiking equipment. My backpack, a day's worth of sample collecting equipment, five Mylar bags. Ouch! Don't bother wiping my face. Is my cheekbone broken?' I hadn't really felt it until then. It must have been the adrenaline keeping the pain at bay.

'Sorry, I didn't mean to hurt you. It looks that way.' Jake put the muddy towel in a laundry bag and opened his comlink. 'Why don't you lie down now? I want to start sorting out the films I shot with my vidcam. Go on, get in your bed. I'll get the medbot set up.'

'Did you film a mammoth?'

'We didn't see any animals today, but I got some nice shots of the area. Why don't you let the medbot put you to sleep while it operates on you? I'll wake you up as soon as we contact Captain Hackab to let him know you're safe. He must be frantic.'

'I'll sleep if you promise not to leave me,' I said, and couldn't hide the tremor in my voice.

He turned around and stared at me. 'You almost sound human, Robin. Did . . . did anything happen between you and Hackab?' He frowned and leaned closer to me. 'I was getting some very strange impressions from Santiago.'

Paranoia is a useful thing. What if Brett were listening? A hidden cam – nothing easier. I hadn't had time to check my vidcam's recordings of what had gone on today in my tent. I gave a shaky laugh. 'Only the usual. He gave orders, march here, sit there, be quiet. I did what he said, and then I fell off a cliff. I was just the *bèn dàn* who fell off a *putain* cliff. Do you realize how stupid I feel?' I didn't get to hear an answer, because at that moment the medbot's anaesthesia kicked in and I fell asleep.

Five hours later, I woke up feeling groggy. The campsite was quiet. I heard a soft snoring and saw Jake, still fully clothed, sprawled on his cot. My head cleared and I sat up. My stomach growled, and I realized I was starving. I crept over to my supplies and grabbed a self-heating meal pack. I didn't check to see what it was. Part of the fun of meal packs was trying to guess what the tasteless mush could be. I squeezed it a couple times, then opened it and sucked on the valve. Could be fish. Or maybe vegetable surprise. Or bug protein. Or seaweed. These days, anything was possible. I didn't look at the label. That would be cheating. Finally, I peeked. Turkey supreme. I never would have guessed.

Using my comlink, I scanned for any hidden vidcams, and as I suspected, there was one in the corner. It was facing my lab, in the back of the tent, but it didn't follow me when I moved, and I saw it had been turned off. Brett had left it there though. It was probably set to activate in the morning.

I called up my floating screen and checked my vidcam's tapes. They showed Brett coming into the tent, examining my lab, and checking my medbot. As I suspected, he took the memory stick out and read it. Then shrugged and put it back. *Nothing to see, sha bi*, I thought angrily.

Then he went through my belongings. He took everything out of my pack, and he went through my comlink files, *nothing there either, sha bi*. I'd been sure to leave only boring notes on the trip, the results of the samples from the wolves, and ideas about the samples I was expecting to get. He examined all my clothes and even held a pair of my underpants to his nose and sniffed. I made a mental note to kill him slowly. Then he hid his spycam in the corner of my tent and went back outside.

I felt rested and strangely calm. I called my little medbot and had it put Jake into a deep slumber. Then I sent it off to Santiago's tent and made sure he was put under as well. As for Brett, I had other plans for him that night.

Humming, I took the vial of smilodon urine I'd collected from when it attacked me. I left the tent, went to the safety perimeter, and deactivated a section so I could leave. I waited a few seconds, and sure enough, Brett lifted the flap of his tent and poked his head out. He'd been watching my tent.

'Where are you going?' he asked in a low voice.

I yawned and stretched, then rubbed my eyes. 'I just woke up. I feel much better. But I have to use the latrine. Did Captain Hackab make it back while I was asleep? I hope he wasn't too worried about me.'

Brett made a strangled noise and shook his head. 'Santiago didn't find him. He won't answer our calls. He's still out there. I don't understand.'

'That *is* odd. He told me he has a tracer,' I said. 'It should be easy to locate him.'

Brett shook his head. 'I have his trace, but he only followed the stream a short way. Then he headed into the valley and kept going west. Santiago didn't want to stay out after dark. He has been trying to raise him by comlink. But all we have is Hackab's tracer – it's moving, so he's still alive.'

'Maybe he thinks he's tracking me?' I wondered aloud. To myself I thought, *one of the wolves swallowed the tracer and is leading these bèn dàns on a merry chase.*

'I don't know.' Brett stepped out of the perimeter. 'I better come with you. There may be dangerous animals around.'

'No, it's safe. Look.' I showed him my floating screen with my vidcam's infrared. From above, Brett and I were two bright green spots. Jake and Santiago were paler green forms lying in their beds – their body heat diffused by the tents. Around us, I could see nothing alarming.

'No, I think it's better I keep watch over you,' he said and fell into step beside me As we walked downhill, I sent the vidcam ahead to scout, but stopped it at the edge of the treeline.

'Why don't you scan further in?' he asked.

'My vidcam has a limited range and the wind is picking up. Did you notice? I don't want to lose it. If it gets blown into the forest, it might get stuck in a tree. Even my floating screen is wavering in the wind, making it hard to read. You can go back. I won't be long. You must be tired.'

'I'm fine. Alloweth me to accompany thee,' Brett said.

'Ah, versed in the latest fad,' I said. 'I wonder if it will last.'

'Methinks it's a valorous way to receiveth people interested in ancient history,' said Brett.

I thought it was a great way to exasperate people, but I simply said, 'If you insist.' I hurried to the latrine and used it, after asking Brett to stand guard. 'Behind the boulder over there, please,' I said. When I finished, I said, 'I'm still covered with mud. I'm going to take a swim in the river. You watch the screen, and if anything appears, let me know.'

Brett glanced at my floating screen, where nothing but our green silhouettes showed. 'Sure. Hold on, let me get a gun. I'd rather be armed if we go down the hill to the meadow.'

'If it makes *you* feel safer,' I said with a shrug, and set off down the hill.

'I guess your screen will show us if there's any danger,' he said, but he looked nervous.

'The wolves move in a pack, and Captain Hackab said that when you men explored yesterday, you discovered they were not in the area.'

'That's true. But there could be smilodons around, or bears.'

'Or giant beavers.'

That made Brett laugh. 'Now, that wouldn't scare me,' he said.

I grinned in the dark. 'I didn't think so. Whoops, sorry, I tripped.' I grabbed his arm, and at the same time, made sure I squirted a good dose of smilodon urine on his pant legs. He didn't notice. It wasn't a strong scent. But it would definitely attract the attention of any animal downwind from us. And right now, we were downwind from the forest and like I'd said, the wind was picking up.

Clouds scudded across the sky. Even at night, because the air was so clean, the stars and moon cast an incredible amount of light. When the clouds covered the moon, it was like hiding the sun. Our shadows disappeared and our surroundings became indistinct. When the clouds moved away, moonlight bathed everything in silver.

To keep Brett occupied, I stripped in front of him, teasingly giving him my clothes to carry for me. I kept my underwear on. There were limits to how far I'd go. I also moved the vidcam so it kept our two glowing silhouettes on the screen but would no longer show anything coming out of the forest.

Felids don't usually like water. Of the modern-day big cats, only tigers and jaguars will willingly plunge into deep water for a swim. I was guessing that the smilodon would be reluctant to swim. In fact, the way it was built, with an extremely muscular neck and forelegs plus a particularly massive bone structure, meant that it probably shunned water. Its teeth would make holding its head out of the water and breathing a problem. I felt safe as I walked down the sloping, muddy shore to the edge of the river and waded in. I noted where the drop-off to deeper water was, and stayed where it was about waist deep. And I kept an eye out for giant beaver, using my vidcam to scan the river behind me.

'You know, Brett, the rising wind is making my vidcam hard to control, and my floating screen is pretty much useless. I'm shutting it down.' I pressed my comlink and the screen vanished.

'Robin?' Brett's voice came out of the darkness. 'I'm going to go get my gun. We should have protection. You stay here, I'll be right back. Don't leave the water until I get back.'

'You're right, Brett,' I said. 'Why don't you put my clothes down, I'll wait until you're back.'

'Are you sure?'

'Yes.' Of course I was sure. He wanted me dead, so leaving me here would probably rate among the things he wanted to do most. If an animal got me, so much the better. I was just glad he didn't have a gun already. He'd have probably shot me in the water, dropped my clothes on the ground, and told everyone he hadn't seen me leave the campsite. But if he wanted to kill me, he'd better act fast. He'd most likely run up, grab his gun, and shoot me. Then he'd make it look like I'd been swept downriver. Maybe he'd even jump in and claim he'd tried to save me.

'I'll be right back,' he repeated. 'Stay put.' He put my clothes down and started back to the base camp. I got out and put my vidcam and screen back on. Brett was no technician. I'd easily programmed the screen to seem shredded by the wind, but the breeze was in no way strong enough to bother it. I turned the vidcam to the forest, and was delighted to see a large shape at the edge. It was the smilodon. He'd caught a whiff of the scent I'd put on Brett's pants. Any minute now, he'd start stalking.

And my favourite creature, the glyptodon, had also come out of the forest. He was now heading uphill towards the tents to try to flirt with one. Now that there were four tents, I imagined the glyptodon would be ecstatic. A harem! I checked the screen and tried to calculate how soon Brett would bump into the glyptodon. He'd

112

probably think it was a boulder. In the dark, it would be hard to tell the difference. I whispered under my breath, 'Three, two, one . . .'

'Hey! What the – Robin? Are you there? What is – oh, it's a glyptodon.' Brett knew what it was. He'd been here before. He laughed and I saw him stop to admire it from a safe distance.

'Do you want me to come?' I called, as I eased out of the water and lay down in the mud, rolling to cover my body in it, all the while keeping an eye on the image of the smilodon on my floating screen. The huge cat ignored my scent, now mostly river water and mud, and concentrated on Brett.

'No, stay there, I'll be right back.' Brett started back up the hill.

In the dark, and in the tall grass, the big cat was invisible. But the glyptodon scented it. He raised his head and trumpeted his alarm.

The smilodon, hearing that and possibly thinking its prey would flee, dropped any pretence of stealth and bounded towards Brett. In ten long leaps it was upon him. Brett didn't know what hit him. The smilodon knocked Brett flat on his back, then, with its powerful front legs, pinned him to the ground, face up. It opened its mouth wide, its huge, curved teeth shining in the moonlight, then it arched its back and drove its teeth into Brett's skull, Brett's face completely hidden in the monstrous cat's gaping mouth. He never even got the chance to scream.

I picked up my clothes and, keeping the glyptodon between me and the smilodon, hiked back to camp. Then I got Brett's gun and a shovel, and I tossed them close to the latrine. The glyptodon followed me everywhere like a tame igloo. It ignored the smilodon, busy chewing on Brett, and only stopped following me when I went back inside the perimeter. For a while, the glyptodon stayed outside, mooing softly at the tents. Finally it grew tired of its one-sided love affair and trotted off down the hill.

I'd always wondered how sabre-toothed tigers killed their prey. Now I knew a little more. Too bad I couldn't have filmed that for the museum. Humming, I wiped my vidcam's memory and put it away and made sure I hadn't left any footprints around. Then I went back to the tent and got the muddy towel out of the laundry bag and

113

used it to clean myself off. The sky was starting to turn grey when I finally crawled back into bed. I would have loved to snuggle up next to Jake, but as I had gone to sleep in my own bed, it would be hard to explain my waking up in his. Exhaustion washed over me. I'd used up the last of my energy. The medbot's healing had worked wonders, but it couldn't help me catch up on my sleep. I needed rest. I only hoped Santiago or Jake wouldn't scream too loudly when they discovered Brett's remains. I wanted to get at least three hours' sleep.

'Wake up! Robin, wake up!' Jake shook my shoulder and I moaned.

'What? Go away. Let me sleep.'

'Robin! Brett was eaten last night by a sabre-toothed tiger!'

Now was my cue to act surprised. *Merde*. I didn't have the energy. 'Go away. I don't believe you.'

'Robin! I'm serious! Get up!'

I rolled over and frowned at him. 'Eaten by a smilodon?' I sat up and groped for my clothes. 'How did it happen? When? Why? Where? Are you sure?' What other questions would a totally innocent person ask, I wondered.

Jake was too distraught to note my less than stellar performance. 'We found his remains near the latrine. He must have gone out last night alone. I told him not to ever leave the campsite at night unless he was accompanied.'

'Maybe Santiago went with him,' I said.

Jake frowned. 'He says not.'

'Didn't you hear a scream or anything?' I barely stifled a yawn and tried to look more concerned. 'How terrible,' I managed.

Jake rubbed his hand over his face. 'We still can't contact Captain Hackab. According to his tracer, he's near the valley where you were yesterday. Last night he moved west, but this morning he changed direction. I think he's still in an area that's blocking radio transmission, but he's heading back to base camp.'

'That's good news,' I said brightly. It was good news. I needed to find out which wolf had eaten Hackab's capsule, so I could try to

114

recover it before the poor animal dissolved. I'd tranquillize it and say I was getting samples. 'Let's go out and meet him. That way, we can find out what happened. He may be injured. Santiago can stay in the base camp today.'

As I expected, Jake didn't agree. 'I need to get the mammoth film done. I'll go to the other side of the river by myself. You go find Captain Hackab with Santiago.'

'Are you sure you'll be safe on your own? Can't you stay at the campsite, or come with us?'

'I will be fine. I won't take any chances, and I'm not planning on getting close to any animals. I'll be sitting in a tree blind and filming with my vidcams. I'll take Brett's cams as well. He . . .' His voice trailed off, and he drew a deep breath. 'We really fucked this up. Tempus U will put us on their blacklist for ever.'

And just wait until they find out that Donnell dissolved and Captain Hackab is being digested by a pack of dire wolves. Aloud, I said, 'I'll have to get another kit together, it will just take me a minute. Is Santiago ready to leave?'

'As soon as you are.' Jake gave me a strange look. 'Do you want to see Brett's remains?'

'I can study them later. After all, he's not going anywhere.' I was having a hard time acting normal. Jake's expression told me I'd gone over some invisible line.

'You act as if you don't care,' he said coldly.

'I do, but I didn't know him very well, and—'

'He was part of the team! There are only four of us now, and you're making jokes like, like – like you don't feel anything!'

I tried to arrange my expression into one that reflected sympathy and lowered my voice to a more sombre tone. 'That's not true, Jake. We should first have a ceremony, don't you think? I mean, before starting to examine him and doing a report.'

Jake nodded. 'You're right. I wasn't thinking straight. The shock of finding him like that . . .'

'Before Santiago and I leave, we'll hold a death ceremony for Brett.' The last death ceremony I'd attended had been for Yasmine.

115

I shivered, and my face must have reflected my distress, because Jake thawed completely. He reached out, pulled me into his arms and hugged him. 'I'm sorry for being such a *wang ba*. I'm having a hard time here. I didn't want to go back in time. My father insisted. Said I had to come back to make sure you were all right.'

I pulled back. 'Your father?'

'And my mother. You should have heard her. "If anything happens to Robin, Jake!" ' he mimicked, and grinned wryly. 'Sometimes I think my parents like you more than they like me.'

'Oh, sibling rivalry now? Is that it?' I grinned and then kissed him. 'Does that mean you're into incest?'

He kissed me back, and then pressed his face to the crook of my neck. His breath was hot on my skin. 'I guess so. I was scared, Robin. I'm fine facing down charging rhinos, lions, rampaging elephants – but I don't know these animals. They are unpredictable. I wouldn't have thought a smilodon would attack someone on open ground – they are slow. They can't run fast. They're supposed to jump on their prey from above. And Brett was armed, had a flashlight with him, even a personal body alarm. He didn't have the time to set anything off. The smilodon just attacked. Animals don't usually do that, especially not for prey they've never seen before.'

'Maybe he was, um, busy on the latrine?' I suggested. *Personal body alarm?* I didn't know that. Thank goodness the smilodon had attacked quickly and Brett had been distracted by the glyptodon.

'No. He was standing up, facing the animal. And that's another thing. He was facing the animal.'

'And that's unusual?'

'Yes, big cats prefer a surprise attack from behind or from overhead. This cat saw Brett and pounced. The only thing I can imagine is that the smilodon was stalking other prey when Brett crossed his path.'

I pretended to think, while packing my kit. 'Maybe the smilodon was just going to the river to drink and Brett was on his territory. Maybe we should move the latrine position.'

'First thing I did,' said Jake. 'After I took care of Brett's remains.'

116

I stopped packing and went to hug him. He was having a hard time with this, and I wished I could help him. If I could, I'd say, *'That sha bi wang ba tried to kill me so I sprinkled him with male smilodon urine. I did that, knowing that smilodons, like most cats, would be fiercely territorial, and that the urine I used wasn't pure – I spiked it with a powerful hormone so that any cat in the area would want to rip his head off.'* But I didn't say that. I just put my kit down and hugged him hard, and said, 'Let's hold the ceremony now. He'd like that.'

We stood around the makeshift autopsy table – a flat rock – Jake, Santiago, me, and the medbot. The little bot had tried desperately to revive Brett, and failing that, had taken to chirping miserably, moving its antennae as if waving the white flag. I was surprised it hadn't covered Brett with a Technicolor cast. The body, I noted, was in two parts. The head, untouched except for two gaping holes in the base of his skull, and the body, which had been eviscerated. Arms and legs more or less intact. Soft tissue gone. I made a mental note to watch the smilodon eat next time. How did he manage with his sabre teeth?

We finished the ceremony – with me wondering about the smilodon's eating habits, Santiago frowning and giving more attention to his comlink than to Brett's body, and Jake acting both angry and worried. I thought I knew why he was so worried. He kept looking at me, and I could tell he was debating whether or not to tell me to stay at the base camp. In the end, he said nothing, because Santiago, with a last look at his comlink, said, 'We have to go. Captain Hackab's tracer just left the valley and is heading this way. But he's moving erratically. He may be injured.'

'Should I bring my medbot?' I asked, stooping to pat the spider-shaped bot.

'No, it's too heavy.' (Santiago was right, it weighed 15 kilos stripped down to the bare necessities – not counting the material it needed to operate, make casts, and mix medicines.)

'Let's go then.' I put my backpack on (my last backpack, if I lost this one I would be in trouble) and picked up a machete.

'Where did you get that?' Santiago frowned.

'Captain Hackab's tent. I'm not proficient with guns, but I want to have some sort of protection. You have a gun, right?' I pointed to the huge rifle strapped across his back. I recognized it as a Maha rifle – with a magnetic flux generator to fire a projectile and three-eyed precision-guided system. He also had a stun gun that could fire in a 20-degree arc with a nine-metre range – and you didn't want to be in that arc when that stun gun went off. I've had people ask why we don't take laser weapons on time-travel trips, and that's an easy one to answer. Energy. We have limited supplies of energy with us, and laser and electromagnetic weapons would drain our batteries in five minutes. We need our batteries for the safety perimeters, the medbots, the comlinks, the vidcams, and for testing, cold storage, etc. Nothing to spare, so we rely on outdated, but still deadly and efficient, weapons.

'I have this too.' He lifted his vest and showed me a holster with what looked like an antique handgun.

I nodded. 'I feel much safer.' But I didn't put my machete down. I didn't feel safer. The rifle strapped to his back would take precious seconds to unstrap and charge, and the pistol was beneath his clothes – panic would not make it easier to reach beneath protective vest and shirt.

After a slight hesitation, Santiago jerked his chin at me. 'Let's go.'

I turned and waved at Jake. 'I have my vidcam this time and we can stay in touch with comlink.' I pointed to my wrist. He didn't look reassured. I knew why – there were too many areas the signal didn't get through.

Back down the hill we went. Past the boulders, past the small cairn marking Donnell's remains. Past the old latrine pit. (The new one was much closer to our base camp. Not ideal, but it showed the extent of Jake's preoccupation.) We reached the meadow, with the river on our left-hand side. It curved left around the base of the cliff then went winding right in a huge 'S' shape before flowing into the forest of giant spruce.

From where we stood, in the meadow, with the grass up to our waists, we couldn't see the marsh, far to our right. On our left, across the river, the giant spruce towered, blocking the view of the low hills behind them. Straight ahead was the oak and pine forest, with the high ridges blue in the distance. Behind the ridges were the deep valleys, where Captain Hackab had tried to kill me. I frowned in thought. Brett and Hackab had acted together on the plan to kill me. So, where did Santiago fit in with all this? I wasn't sure yet. I kept my machete in my hand as we crossed the meadow and entered the dappled shade under the trees.

Chapter Fourteen

This was nearer than I wanted to be to the smilodon territory. I would have preferred to go further to the right, near the swamp, where the mud and water would discourage the big, heavy cat from attacking. Here, under the trees, I was nervous despite my vidcam that I set to hover overhead just above the trees, with my floating screen as close as I could get it. But we were moving too fast, and for that system to work best, we should be letting the vidcams move ahead. When I mentioned this to Santiago, he looked back over his shoulder at me and said, 'We're pressed for time.'

I checked his floating screen – he had Captain Hackab's tracer – and saw the red dot was moving towards us. If we kept up this pace the wolves would meet us in under an hour. My hand tightened on the machete.

Santiago set a blistering pace; luckily the forest was mostly devoid of underbrush. The ground was hard-packed dirt littered with dead leaves and the occasional white bone. A fire had gone through here not long ago, maybe a year or so – the lower branches of the pines were singed black stumps, charred wood lay in heaps, and bright green new growth crowded into each sunlit clearing. I insisted on stopping and examining the bones we came across. Most belonged to small rodents, a few were deer, and I noted the marks of teeth and claws on the larger bones. I pretended great interest, when all I was doing was buying time to rest.

'This must have been killed by the smilodon, but as you can see, the wolves finished the carcass. The bones are –' I looked up, but

Santiago was not listening. He frowned impatiently and motioned for me to hurry. I dropped the bone, brushed my hands on my pants, and set off at a jog.

'So, Santiago, what did you and Donnell talk about on Mars?' I asked. Might as well get everything out in the open.

'Nosy girls don't last long,' he said, not breaking pace.

'You don't sound surprised.'

'You take me for a *bèn dàn*?' He laughed. 'You'll have to tell me how Donnell got killed by a pack of mangy wolves when he was the best survival expert I ever knew. Except Hackab, who will be one fucking surprised *wang ba* when he sees you.'

'Really?' I was panting, trying to keep up.

'The girl with nine lives. That's what I've decided to call you.'

'Why?' I stumbled over a root, caught myself, and hurried after him.

'I know a lot about you, Robin Johnson. I know you spent your formative years in a psychiatric ward, and there is no way you should have been chosen to go on this trip, or any trip for that matter. I don't understand how you got here. Dr Powell should have vetoed it.' For the first time, his voice reflected emotion, and it sounded like anger.

'Because I'm an expert in typhus. Not that I know anything about this new disease. And Dr Powell did try to stop me,' I admitted.

'What did you do to Dr Powell to make him so attached to you? Does his wife know about you two?'

'Not Dr Powell, Jake,' I said, not rising to his bait.

'Pretty boy Jake. If he's lucky he'll make it back to Tempus U in one piece, instead of several – like poor Brett. For some reason, I can't seem to imagine him just standing there while a smilodon jumped on him.'

'And yet, that's what seems to have happened,' I said. I caught up to Santiago and checked the screen again. The wolves were not even a kilometre away. In ten minutes they'd be on us. 'He wasn't an expert on wild animals, or on survival. He should have stayed in his lab, making viruses and getting the antibodies.'

'Yes, I figured you knew about all that. Donnell must have had an *"open in case of my death"* file. Is that it?'

I ignored that question as well and said, 'Too bad instead of just making the animals and humans sick, the virus killed most of them. There isn't a camel, or a horse, or an elk moose left. And there were humans too, weren't there? You killed them all with your greed. It's going to be hard to bring back any antibodies when there aren't any survivors. You'll never recoup your losses. Especially when I tell everyone how it all started.'

'Don't worry about my losses. I don't need a bunch of animals. Brett gave me a dose of specially treated Typhus-77, as everyone has started to call it. We gave it to your pretty boy before we time-travelled By the time we go back, he should be either sick or dead, and either way we get our antibodies. I can see the headlines. Time traveller brings back cure for Typhus-77 from the past. Hackab and I will split two ways what should have been four. I think I should thank you, Robin, for increasing my profits.'

My mind raced. *Jake was infected with the virus?* 'Thank me? You think I had something to do with Donnell's death? Or Brett's?'

'Donnell I don't know, but Brett – definitely. You probably lured him out of the campsite with some sort of promise – was it sex? And the smilodon was just serendipity. Otherwise, we probably never would have found him. Admit it. You're just like your father, you like killing.'

When I could get my voice under control I said, 'Aren't you scared of me?'

'What? You and your machete? I have body armour covering all my vital organs. You can't hurt me. Try it – just try.' Santiago stopped and stood, holding his arms out. 'Come on. I'll make it easy – I'll kneel down and you can try to cut off my head. Or aim for a major artery.'

'Don't be a *bèn dàn*,' I said. I could see the faint glow the body armour made. It encased him from his head to mid-thigh. And he wore high boots, most likely reinforced with armour as well.

'Not many people call me an idiot and get away with it,' he said, looking at his floating screen. 'Hackab is just over that ridge. I'll tell you what. I won't kill you right away. Let's pretend I feel bad about killing you, so I'll give you a head start. I'll count to thirty. You can run in whichever direction you want.'

'You're sick.'

'Ten-second penalty for every insult. Now it's twenty seconds.'

I looked at him and lifted my lips in a primitive snarl. 'Turn around and close your eyes. Count loud enough that I can hear you,' I said.

He started to laugh and turned his back to me, but I saw him slide his stun gun from its holster. 'One, two –'

I swung my machete with all my force. I didn't want to kill him. I didn't aim for a vital organ. I aimed for the back of his knees and cut as deeply as I could, severing his hamstrings. He toppled to the ground, screaming, and fired. I was just outside the arc, but I still felt my muscles tetanize and it took all my strength to keep my legs moving.

'Run, Robin! Run as fast as you can. Hackab will kill you. Stupid bitch. You ruined everything! I should have killed you when I had the chance!' He ended on a scream and a high-velocity bullet smashed through a tree on my left. I didn't look back. I dodged left, and Santiago, thinking I would jump right, missed again. I put on a last burst of speed and plunged over a high bank, rolling down the far side and coming to rest against a thick tree trunk.

'*Merde*,' I gasped. I got up, called my floating screen to show the way back to camp, and started to run. Santiago shot two more bullets at me before giving up. With a severed hamstring, he couldn't walk. As soon as the wolves found him, they'd have another feast. He'd better save some ammunition. I half wished I could see his face when Captain Hackab's tracer arrived – in the belly of a dire wolf.

I didn't want to risk going through the forest, so I cut back to my left now, where the swamp was. I kept to the edges, and called Jake on my comlink.

'Robin? Is that you?' he said. 'Did you find Captain Hackab? How is he?'

123

'Yeah, it's me. Change of plans. Santiago met Captain Hackab. They, uh, found the wolves and want to get samples. I have a feeling they're going to start shooting. Jake, Santiago had live ammo with him, and I didn't want to be part of that. I told them I was heading back, and they had no choice but to agree.'

'That's good.'

'Jake, how are you feeling? I need to know.'

'I don't feel so great, but it's nothing. I'll meet you back at camp.' He sounded distracted.

'Are you going to be all right? Do you want me to come get you?'

'Just a strange headache. It might be a leftover from the time sickness. I'll meet you back at camp. If you could set your vidcam up near the edge of the forest before coming in, we can get some footage of the smilodon for the museum. If Santiago and Hackab have enough samples, you can spend the rest of the week processing them while I try to get some good films.'

'Where are you exactly?'

I tapped in his comlink number to get a location for him.

'I'm in a tree.' He sounded faintly surprised. 'And my nose is bleeding.'

'Jake! Turn your vidcam on you so I can see you. Can you hear me?'

'My nose is bleeding?' He coughed. 'I really don't feel so good.'

'I'm on my way. Don't move.' I started running in earnest. 'Can you keep talking to me? Tell me where you are? Jake!'

'Don't worry, I'll just lie down for a bit.' His voice trailed off.

I dropped the machete, shrugged out of my backpack, tore off my jacket and vest and threw them aside, all the while running as fast as I could. Lighter now, I picked up speed. I'd wanted to stay close to the swamp, but the soft ground would slow me down. I had to reach Jake, but I needed Yah. My plan was to first go to his cave, then try to make him understand I'd need his help to carry Jake if Jake couldn't walk. And not only to help me carry – I needed his blood.

As I ran, I screamed. 'Yah! Yah!' I'd hit my stride – pounding over the hard ground, jumping over fallen branches and dodging stumps, arms pumping, screaming. I sent my vidcam ahead to scout, and my floating screen was hard put to keep up with me. But I kept it on, I didn't want to run into a smilodon. I needn't have worried. Perhaps my screams scared it, but there was nothing in the woods that day – only the pack of wolves far behind me, and they had just met Santiago. I heard the report of a rifle – only one – and then nothing.

I reached the meadow soon after, and I kept screaming, 'Yah!' I found the path leading to the cliff base and kept running, although it was more of a jog now, I caught my breath, then ran again, then slowed to rest. In between bursts of speed I tried to call Jake but he wasn't answering. I had his location though. He was on the other side of the river.

'Yah!' Rounding a corner, I ran smack into him. He had been running towards me. Luck would have us meet at the corner of the biggest clump of sedge grass in the area, hiding each other from view. I picked myself up, rubbed my skinned knee, and grabbed his hand. 'Come!' I said, and started towards my base camp.

He followed willingly, and when we reached the camp, he went straight to my tent and grabbed a meal pack. He was also thrilled when I rummaged beneath my bed and tossed him his spear. He was less thrilled when I told the medbot to take blood from him, and it took all my chocolate bars shoved into his arms to persuade him to sit still for the bot.

Meanwhile, I put his blood into another lab bot, one that was designed especially to create a vaccine from antibodies. I knew that in the early days of vaccination, passive immunity was induced artificially when antibodies were given as a medication to a non-immune individual. All I had to do was pool and purify Yah's blood and give as big a dose as possible to Jake. The protection offered by passive immunization was short-lived, usually lasting only a few weeks. But it would protect Jake right away and hopefully help fight the virus already in his system.

'Hurry, hurry,' I begged, as I paced. Yah, to his credit, had only eaten one meal pack but he'd already devoured five chocolate bars and was about to open another one. I thought he'd probably be sick, and motioned for him to stop.

He immediately grabbed the rest of the chocolate and clutched it to his chest.

'Yes, *Ahoh, ahoh*, it's all yours. Don't worry. But you have to help me. *Shika* – help. I need *shika* with my family – my *adeez*.'

Yah put the chocolate down and said, '*Ish shika adeez nika a shwao*.'

I had no idea what he'd just said, but he picked up his spear and headed out the tent-flap, pausing to wait for me. I took a deep breath, put the purified blood into three different injectors (I'd seen too many holofilms where someone loses the only vial of antidote) and followed Yah.

Yah must have spent his time watching the base camp carefully. He seemed to know exactly where Jake had gone, and when we passed the place where Brett had been killed, he pointed with his spear and said something like '*Ako nashdotso*'. He paused, peering closely at me, as if demanding a reply.

I figured it meant that the smilodon had been there, and I nodded. 'Yes – *ahoh* – he ate someone who wanted to kill me, so we're not sad. In fact, we're pretty happy about it.'

Yah looked impressed, but I couldn't say why. There was still too much of a gulf between us. We had arrived at a sort of basic communication, but it wasn't sophisticated enough to share much more than the words *yes, help, family*, and the names of some animals.

We waded across the river, after looking carefully in all directions. I showed Yah my floating screen, to prove to him there were no animals around, but all he wanted to do was poke it. He hadn't made the connection between what was on the screen and his surroundings. Once on the other side of the river, we crossed a large expanse of mud, tangled roots, and fallen trees. The giant spruce forest was harder to navigate than the scrub oak forest on our side of the river, but this was mammoth territory and the great beasts had made well-worn paths through the trees. Signs of mammoth were the many huge piles of dung, white scars on the trees where branches had been torn down, and bark ripped off the trees. The tree got bigger as the ground got higher and dryer and there was more space to move. The mammoths liked to go to the river's edge to graze on the sedge grass and the smaller, more tender trees and their branches. Near the riverside, the trees were slender and stunted, and the ground was marshy with stagnant ponds thick with algae.

As we advanced and the terrain rose above the waterline, the trees seemed to stretch and reach for the sky. When we reached the oldest part of the forest the light grew dimmer, greener, and sounds were muted.

Yah stopped and made a sign of respect to the trees. He touched his chest with his fist and raised his gaze to the treetops. For once, I knew what he felt. These trees had stood for hundreds of years, and some were truly immense. Most trunks were covered with moss, and thick moss covered the ground. Sometimes whole trees had fallen, and wherever a shaft of light reached the forest floor, fern grew in pale green, delicate bunches.

I checked my floating screen and located Jake. He wasn't far. I couldn't raise him on the comlink though. Finally, after what seemed like hours, we reached a small clearing. Several huge trees had fallen, knocking a hole in the canopy that let in floods of sunlight. I saw the tree-blind built on one of the more massive trees, on the far side. It looked like a tent – same igloo shape, only this time set up on a platform high above the ground. Of course it had to be high – the mammoths were four metres tall, and with their trunks, could easily reach ten metres high. But unless a mammoth decided to knock the tree down, the blind was safe. Yah stopped and stared at the blind.

'Jake?' I called. Getting no answer, I made my way through the tangle of fallen branches, climbed over a mossy trunk, and started up the ladder, motioning to Yah to follow me. He hesitated, glanced behind him, and carefully climbed up after me.

Jake had crawled to the back of the blind and lay on his side. The only light in the blind came from the film studio he'd set up, and I noticed his vidcams were still in action, filming a troop of mammoths heading our way. I would have liked to stop and watch them, but Jake came first. While Yah stood and gaped at the many floating screens, I

127

knelt by Jake and carefully turned him over. He was unconscious, his skin hot and dry, with blood smeared across his face from a recent nosebleed. I activated my vitapak and took the three injections I'd tucked in my ankle pack and belt. My vitapak turned an angry orange-red, and I used my comlink to connect it to my floating screen. Immediately it started listing everything that needed attention – in short, I needed to get him to my medbot as soon as possible.

I injected all three samples into him. One into a vein, the other two into muscle – one behind his shoulder, the other in the thigh. I took a risk with the intravenous injection – but I couldn't wait. It would take at least an hour for the intramuscular shots to start diffusing into his system, and I needed his body to react. I'd added the old antibiotic that used to be given, although with this new strain, its effectiveness was practically nil. I'd also included a hefty dose of cortisone and vitamin K, all the while praying he wouldn't die, because his parents would never forgive me. I was starting to realize just how much Dr Powell and his wife, Jeannie, meant to me. I hadn't let myself get close to anyone, but somehow they'd gotten close anyhow. I wiped angry tears out of my eyes and said, 'Jake Powell, if you die on me I'll never forgive you.'

He stirred and without opening his eyes he said, 'Robin? Is that you?'

'No, it's the Blue Fairy, here to grant you a wish.' I brushed a lock of sweat-soaked hair off his forehead. 'As soon as you can get up, we have to go back to the base camp.'

'I don't know if I'll make it,' he said.

'Don't be a fu—'

'Don't swear at me, Robin. You have to learn to watch that mouth of yours.' He stopped talking, out of breath. He coughed, and a trickle of blood appeared at the corner of his mouth. 'Got a good film of the mammoths. You should see them. It was worth the trip just to see them. Magnificent . . .' He tried to breathe, shuddered, and lapsed into unconsciousness again.

Yah appeared at my side and looked at Jake. He poked my arm. '*Adeez*?' He asked.

'Yes, Jake is my family. *Adeez*,' I confirmed. I looked closer at Yah. Although he was incredibly strong, he was definitely not strong enough to carry Jake back to the camp. But he might be able to save him. 'Yah – listen to me. This is important. I need you to get my medbot and carry it to me, but you can't get it wet. Look.' I took his chin in one hand and pointed to my floating screen. 'Show medbot,' I ordered, and the bot appeared on the screen.

Yah flinched, but I kept my grip on his chin. 'Look,' I insisted. 'Show a man carrying the medbot,' I ordered, and the screen obliged by showing a lab technician walk over, pick up the medbot and hold it carefully. 'Show how to keep a medbot from getting wet in waist-deep water,' I said, praying that there was something in the files about that. In fact, there was. A man walked into a stream, holding the medbot out of the water as he crossed from one side to the other.

'Yah, please – go get my medbot and bring it here.' I pointed to the medbot on the screen, then showed Jake.

There was no indication he understood. He didn't nod, or look at the screen again. He put his hand on my mouth, as if to tell me to be quiet. Then he put his hand on his own chest. He got up and left. A second later, he came back and picked up his spear. I thought I saw a grin on his face, and then he ducked out of the blind.

I decided to send a vidcam after him. If he didn't go to the base camp, I'd go myself. I didn't want to leave Jake though. My vitapak still glowed red-orange – although Jake's breathing seemed to have eased somewhat.

I rolled him to his side and put him in the recovery position, and more blood dribbled from his lips. It was bright pink, so I thought maybe his lungs were affected. But there were only a few drops. His skin still felt acid hot, and he didn't respond when I called his name. For a while I just sat and held his hand, stroking his head, and telling him everything was going to be fine. When an hour had passed, I checked Yah's progress and was relieved to see he'd crossed the river and was heading to the base camp. I deactivated the safety perimeter, so he could cross it, and I went back to Jake's side.

Suddenly a crackling sound came from outside and I opened to the tent-flap to look. Through the trees came a herd of mammoths. I'd been prepared to see mammoths, but looking at pictures or films of them and then actually seeing them up close was so different I nearly forgot what I was doing. Their sheer size, strength, and even the *smell* of them was overwhelming. After gaping for a moment, my mouth open, my legs and arms shaking with primal fear, I managed to get hold of myself. I quickly checked to make sure the vidcams were still filming, then I sat at the edge of the blind and watched.

At first I could only catch glimpses of them through the trees as they stopped just outside the clearing. The first mammoth that stepped into the clearing was much larger than I'd expected. Or rather, I knew mammoths were big – I'd seen them at the river, and stood right next to a skeleton in the museum. But this beast was so much more massive than the skeleton – it had bones, and muscles, a layer of fat, and a coat of thick fur. Its fur was amazing – it hung in long dreadlocks from its sides, it curled on its head and tiny ears, and on its back, the fur stood up in a ridge along its backbone that added another fifty centimetres to its height. I wondered if the thick ridge of hair had evolved in response to the smilodon's huge teeth, or if the smilodon's teeth had evolved to cope with the mammoth's thick fur.

This was a Columbian mammoth – the largest of its species. The Columbian mammoth evolved from the steppe mammoth, which entered North America from Asia about 1.5 million years ago. One of the largest mammals to walk the earth, the males measured four metres at the shoulder and must have weighed ten tons. This male ignored me and the tree blind. It raised its trunk and scented the air, but our smell was completely unknown and so wasn't associated with the notion of threat. It peered around the clearing, then, satis- fied, it turned and lifted its trunk and uttered a low rumble. Instantly, the rest of the troop jostled into the clearing and set about using their trunks to tear the low branches from the spruce. The herd was smaller than I'd expected, consisting of a huge bull, three cows, and a calf. A juvenile male hung back, and I supposed he'd be leaving soon. Some raw scars on his side showed where the alpha bull had raked him with its massive tusks.

The mammoths' tusks were fantastic, long, curving ivory, stained green and brown from the vegetation. The male's tusks must have been over four metres long and I'd be hard pressed to put my arms all the way around the base. They tapered to points that had been dulled by constant gouging and scraping, but they were still deadly.

The mammoths' reddish-brown coats were thick and matted, and they smelled both strangely sweet, like honey, and rancid. Their scent mixed with the fresh smell of pine as they broke branches, chewing with exaggerated sideways movements of their jaws, green froth drooling from their mouths. The calf stayed close to its mother. It had a lighter, silkier coat and long, curling eyelashes. The mammoths had amber-coloured eyes, which were larger than modern elephants' eyes.

Clouds of flying insects accompanied the mammoths. When one raised its tail and produced a prodigious pile of manure, I saw why. The insects swarmed over the manure, sucking up the liquid, laying their eggs, or feasting. Other insects harassed the mammoths, getting into their ears, their eyes, and even under their thick fur. The mammoths shook their heads, swished their tails, and rubbed up against the trees in a constant effort to relieve themselves of the itching, biting pests. Their fur was matted with dried mud, and I imagined they had a wallow where they would coat themselves in mud to keep the insects away. One large cow came to the tree where the blind was set up and started rubbing her head against it, her huge tusks on either side of the trunk. As she nodded her head up and down, I could feel the tree move. Six or seven tons of solid mammoth muscle would knock down just about any tree – but she just wanted to scratch her forehead on the rough bark. I could have climbed down a few rungs, reached and touched her, but I didn't. I wasn't alone, Jake was desperately ill, and I didn't want to panic the herd. Besides, the vidcams were still filming, and a modern human arm suddenly appearing in the picture would not please the museum crowd.

The mammoths stayed for a while, eating the new growth that had sprung up in the clearing, stomping on and breaking the fallen tree, and I saw them pulling the tops of the more slender trees towards them in order to reach the more tender branches.

After taking a full gastronomic tour of the clearing, the bull swung around and headed back towards the heart of the forest. The young male quickly moved aside and let the larger mammoth pass. The cow with the calf followed, then the two other females. The young male waited a while, shifting his weight from foot to foot, swinging his trunk and looking undecided. Then he shook himself, like a huge dog, a cloud of dust rising from his thick coat, and followed the rest of the troop. Apparently he still felt part of the family group – although for how long I couldn't tell. Most likely if one of the other cows came into heat the old bull would chase him away for good – or kill him.

I checked on Jake – still no change, the vitapak still a violent red-orange. I made sure the vidcams were still following the mammoths, and that they were programmed to return when the mammoths were out of range. Then a horrible thought struck me and I opened my floating screen to check on Yah. He'd arrived at the camp, and to my relief, he went straight to my tent and picked up the medbot – after poking it a few times with his spear. He carried it gingerly, holding it at arm's' length, and I hoped he wouldn't drop it in the river. I'd deactivated the safety perimeter so he'd been able to get in, and now I used my comlink to reset it so the glyptodon would not trample our tents. The silly beast was just outside the perimeter. It lifted its head when Yah walked by, but went back to grazing and keeping an eye on his harem of tents.

I used the vidcam to scan the area around Yah, but there were no other animals – just the glyptodon. The smilodon and the wolves were elsewhere, and the herd of mammoth had vanished into the forest. I hadn't seen the bear since he'd been at the riverbank fishing for giant salmon, and the beaver . . . I frowned and looked at my screen. The beaver was in the river, on its patrol, and it was headed upstream, swimming strongly, towards the shallow crossing where Yah would soon be. I sent my vidcam buzzing around Yah's head, trying to get his attention, but he only glanced at it and hurried on. I admired his concentration, but I knew I had to distract the beaver.

My floating screen had a range of one kilometre from my comlink, but I could project one from my vidcam as well, so I quickly searched my files for the film of the bear that I'd taken. I projected it onto the screen and sent it downstream. Then I used my vidcam to make the screen dive at the beaver. Annoyed by the flashing light, it lifted its head and spotted the bear on the screen. Modern beavers have poor eyesight but excellent hearing. My floating screen, combined with the vidcam, had sound, so I played the sounds of the bear grunting as it ripped the salmon with its claws.

Confused, the beaver dove underwater. I held my breath. After a minute, the beaver reappeared, this time on the other side of the river and heading back downstream – away from Yah.

Jake made a sound and I knelt by his side. The vitapak was still orange, but the red had faded somewhat. He had stopped sweating, and his breathing sounded clearer. 'Are you awake?' I asked.

'I think so. What is that awful smell?'

'Mammoths. They were in the clearing. They've gone, lie still,' I said, gently pushing him back down. 'Rest. The vidcams got everything and are following them. And my medbot is on its way.'

'Santiago is bringing it?' he asked.

I didn't think he'd ask that. I didn't know what to say, but his eyelashes fluttered and he closed his eyes. Saved by a faint? I checked his vitals. He was not very stable, but if he could hold on until the medbot got here, he might make it back to the base camp, and there I could hook my medbot to him *and* to my lab. *If* we could get him back to the base camp. There were too many ifs. I checked my screen again and saw Yah coming down the mammoth trail, still holding the medbot gingerly – as if it might attack him any minute. I admired his courage. He made an incongruous picture with the high-tech medbot held out in front of him, his spear wrapped in a leather thong and tied to his back. He'd taken off his rabbit fur leggings to cross the stream and wrapped them around his neck like a scarf. Jake would have a fit when he saw him.

I wondered if I could find a jacket or something and disguise Yah as Santiago, who'd been dark-haired. But no, Yah was dark-skinned like me, and his gap-toothed grin was nothing like Santiago's perfectly straight teeth. It cheered me up immensely to think of Santiago's teeth in the belly of a dire wolf.

I climbed down and took the medbot from Yah, who practically threw it at me, then hopped away flapping his hands as if he'd been stung. I wondered why, then I noticed that the medbot did emit a faint vibration because of its battery. I'd never noticed – I was so used to technology. My admiration for Yah increased immensely. I climbed up to the blind and activated the bot. The medbot chirped, beeped, and rushed about Jake, poking and prodding him. Yah watched carefully, and he seemed to understand the bot was trying to help. Finally the bot injected enough meds into him that Jake was able to stagger to his feet. We managed to get him down the ladder with both Yah and me hanging on to him. I went back for the bot, and Yah fixed up a travois with long poles, using the tent flap to make a sling to carry Jake, and we dragged him back to base camp. It was exhausting and harrowing. Jake hallucinated nearly the whole way back. Yah wouldn't hurry. Carrying a wounded person was a screaming advertisement to any predator in the area, so he kept making me stop while he went ahead to check the area. I kept trying to make him use the floating screen, but he ignored it unless he was poking holes in it or making it swirl around with his hand.

I used the pauses to make sure the medbot and Jake were still connected – with all the bumps and jostling, it wasn't easy. The medbot wasn't made to go on safaris although it was tougher than it looked. Get it wet though and we were finished. I unhooked it and held it carefully when we crossed the river. The travois floated beautifully, and Jake woke up in the middle of the river, looked at Yah and me, and gave us an enormous grin.

'This is such an amazing dream,' he said, lifting his hand to point, then letting it drop. He looked startled at the splash, then grinned again and started telling me about the time he and Helen went to the beach and rented a hovercraft.

'Helen is an empty-headed, boring idiot,' I said.

'Do I detect a jealous monster biting you?' Jake asked. 'Oh, look at that sunset. That is just amazing.'

134

It *was* amazing. The hot, dry weather painted the sunset with gaudy reds, pinks, and oranges. Pale dust glittered in the air, our bodies were gilded, and our shadows reached in navy blue stripes across the golden meadow.

'Yes, I guess I'm jealous,' I admitted, but Jake had fallen back asleep. Once we got him to camp, and he was getting treatment, I hiked back to the tree blind and got what equipment I could carry. I left the tent and the heavier things – everything was made to be bio-degradable and would break down in a matter of weeks, even the tent. There wasn't too much else I could do. When I got back, it was fully dark and the moon was rising.

I secured the perimeter, after showing Yah what I was doing and what happened if you crossed it (I set it on the lowest voltage and let him touch it). He jumped back, but then put his hand on his chest again, and I had a feeling that meant '*I understand*'. Yah set his spear against my tent and sat in the doorway, munching on a chocolate bar.

After I made sure Jake was sleeping, I came out and made a camp-fire. Yah and I shared a few insta-meals, and he even let the medbot come and take more blood from him. We finished the evening in comfortable silence. I loved stargazing in this time – the heavens seemed so close. I reached a hand out and pretended to pluck a star, and Yah pointed at the stars and said something. I pointed to the same constellation and said, 'The great bear. Bear, you know. Hold on.' I called up my floating screen and showed him the film I'd made. 'Bear!' I said, pointing at the animal, then at the sky.

Yah looked at the screen, then followed my gaze to the stars. He pointed at the screen, then at the constellation and said, '*Deetoy*'.

'*Deetoy*? That is a bear?' I mimed a bear's shuffling walk and Yah laughed.

'*Ahoh, deetoy. Deetoy asha ipo. Ipo!*' He opened his arms wide and made a swimming motion. '*Ipo!*'

Ipo was salmon, or maybe big fish. The bear eats salmon. I nodded eagerly. '*Asha*? Eat?' I mimed eating.

Yah said, '*Ahoh*,' which meant yes.

'How do you say, moon?' I pointed to the moon.

'*Honay,*' he said.

'*Honay,*' I echoed. I was content. We were slowly starting to communicate. But I was speaking his language, and he wasn't speaking mine. I thought it unfair, so I pointed to the moon and the constellation of the bear again and said, 'Moon. Bear.'

Yah looked at the heavens, and said, 'Moon, *honay.* Bear, *deetoy. Asha,* eat. Robin, *adeez.*' He put his hand on my shoulder. '*Adeez* Yah.'

'Family,' I said. '*Adeez* is family. Yah is Robin's family.' I was touched, but sad. In a few days I'd be gone. I wondered where Yah would go. Were there any other people around? 'Yah, where are other people? *Adeez?*' I pointed to the four Cardinal points and repeated, '*Adeez?*'

Yah grew still and looked at me. '*Doo adeez,*' he said, sweeping his arm in a great arc. He picked up a handful of dirt and showed it to me. Then he stood and, looking at me, he scattered it into the fire. '*Doo adeez,*' he said again.

I understood. The ones he knew, or at least knew about, had been consumed by the funeral pyres. He was alone.

Chapter Fifteen

While I waited for Jake to recuperate, I got busy using Yah's blood to make as many samples as I could. With modern food and vitamins, he had started to gain weight and it suited him. The medbot even fixed his teeth – I had the little bot treat him the next morning and programmed a dental 'makeover' that fixed a couple of cracked molars, replaced his incisor, and gave him a much-needed cleaning.

First, I had the medbot do my teeth, to show Yah what was going to happen. It didn't hurt, but it surprised him, and he got up a couple of times, so the medbot chased him around the campsite. But Yah was mostly agreeable to the treatment. When it was over, he couldn't get over it, peering into my mirror, and grinning and patting the medbot, which had now become his best friend. I imagine the cracked molars had been paining him for a long time.

I finished getting the films of the mammoths and the bear ready. I needed to film the smilodon, so I planned to go out the next day with Yah to set up some vidcams. I'd gotten some good footage of the beaver and the glyptodon as well. The beaver, on its incessant patrol up and down the river, was now easy to avoid – and to film. The glyptodon hardly left our area, and out of pity for him, I took down Santiago's tent and set it up outside the perimeter so the glyptodon could nuzzle it. Everyone needs some company.

The bear didn't reappear, and the salmon were gone as well, so I guessed it was a seasonal migration. The wolves were in the next valley over, and one of my next projects should be to go find them and make sure that the capsules that had been in Santiago and

Hackab had gone through their digestive systems without harming them. I could programme my vidcam to find them without too much difficulty. I'd bag the capsules and bring them back with me. One other thing I did was to take the capsule out of Jake's body too. I didn't trust those things any more. I'd explain everything when I got back.

'Robin?' Jake's voice was weak.

'Hey, there you are. How are you feeling?' I sat next to him and took a look at his vitapak. It was yellow. Not great, but getting better.

'Dizzy. Tired. What happened to me?'

He'd asked this a couple times, but kept forgetting. He'd also been delirious. I thought he looked better today. Maybe he'd be all right now. 'You had Typhus-77. The medbot has been treating you. We gave you some purified blood with antibodies, so your system got a head start fighting, but it's been tough. You lost your spleen, and your white blood cell count is still far too low. Until we can get it up, you're going to be feverish and exhausted, so just rest.' I checked his vitals as I talked. The vitapak glowed yellow, but not orange or red. Progress was slow. The virus had ravaged his body.

'Did I dream, or is there a caveman with us?'

'Not a dream. Yah is very much real. He probably saved your life, so be nice to him.'

'I dreamed so many things, I don't know what's real anymore. Where are Brett . . .' his voice trailed away. 'I forgot. He was eaten by the smilodon. And Santiago, And Captain Hackab?'

'They've left the campsite.' I avoided the truth, figuring Jake didn't need any more stress. 'The virus is highly contagious,' I reminded him.

'Oh.' His frown slid off his face as he tried to stay conscious, but the medbot had decided he needed rest more than anything. Before he went under I bent down and kissed him. 'I'm here, don't worry. Just sleep and get well, Jake.'

'Robin. Wake up. Wake up, Robin, I have to talk to you.'

In my dreams, Yasmine can be remarkably bossy. I was dreaming, I knew I was dreaming because Yasmine was there, perched on the

138

end of my bed, sitting cross-legged, her feet bare (she hated shoes). She was looking at her nails. She was always doing something with her nails – this time they were silver, with a tiny frosting of diamond chips along the edges.

'I have beautiful nails,' she said, wiggling her fingers at me. 'I bet you're jealous.'

'You didn't come all this way to show me your manicure. You know you're over twelve thousand years away from your own birth?' I said. In this dream I was incredibly lucid.

'I have my whole life in front of me. No wonder I feel so alive and strong.' She laughed, and electricity seemed to crackle around her teeth and hair.

'I wish . . .' my voice trailed away.

'You wanted to go back in time and visit me. I know.' Her voice was gentle now. She leaned over and took my hand in hers. 'Listen, Robin. Do you hear anything?'

I shook my head, but then I realized I did hear something. Something faint and far away. 'Dry leaves crackling. Dust. Something dragging? It's a dull, thumping sound. What is it?'

'Santiago isn't dead, Robin. Not until you see him die.'

'He has to be!' I gasped and sat up in bed, and of course I woke up, and of course Yasmine wasn't there. I was alone.

I thought about what my dream meant. In the back of my mind, I must be afraid Santiago had survived. If that was the case, Jake, Yah, and I were still in danger. Santiago would want to kill me, and use Jake and Yah for the antibodies. He'd keep them alive just long enough to get as much blood as he could, then he'd most likely kill them.

I didn't want to leave Jake alone in the campsite, but I had to make sure Santiago was dead. Yah and I set off at dawn the next morning, keeping near the swamp as we headed into the forest. Then Yah headed upland and I followed. The terrain grew rocky, and I recognized part of the valley where the wolves lived.

We still didn't speak the same language, but now I used the screen to communicate. I showed Yah a holo of Santiago and mimed

139

looking for him. I also knew the word for wolf, *makii*, and I managed to tell him I needed to find the wolves. I thought the wolves might be lurking near the spot Santiago had attacked me, and where I'd hamstrung him – but I hadn't been able to locate the exact spot on the map. And I didn't want to stumble on him if there was any chance he was still alive. I tried to explain about Santiago, and how I'd cut his legs, and how dangerous he could be, but it was futile.

Yah scratched his head. Obviously I was crazy, but he shrugged. '*Nashdotso ell makii eko,*' he said, indicating the way we were going.

The smilodon and the wolves were in the same area. I smiled. 'Good – we get two things done in one day. Perfect. Show me where the *nashdotso* is, and I'll set up vidcams with motion sensors.'

What was nice about Yah was that he never argued. He didn't understand half of what I said, but he got the gist of it. I wasn't sure if he connected the vidcam with the screen, but he'd started recognizing the screen as being a holographic image and not a real object, although he still loved to poke at it.

I set up vidcams along a ridge, and then Yah pointed to a cave on the opposite side of the ravine and told me the *nashdotso* lived there, so I sent a vidcam over and sure enough, curled up and asleep deep in a narrow cave, was a magnificent smilodon.

I watched it on the screen, with Yah standing open-mouthed by my side. He kept looking over at the cave, then at the screen. Finally he seemed to get it. Agitated, he pointed at the screen and at the cave, and then he started to run back to the base camp.

I was about to call him back, when I looked at the screen again. The smilodon's eyes were open.

I could run too. Yah and I pelted back to camp, not even slowing down when we got to the safety perimeter. Only once we were inside, and panting, did we look at the screen to see where the big cat was. He was standing on the ridge, where we had been not long before, and he was sniffing the ground.

I kept the vidcams on it, filming, as the cat put its shoulder on the ground, then lay down and rolled over, rubbing its back into our scent. Then it crouched, its huge teeth glinting in the half-light

140

under the trees. Its cold yellow eyes stared out of the screen at us and I shivered.

'Not a good sign, Yah,' I said. 'He's marked us for his own. We better be careful. I think I'll leave Santiago where he is for now. I'll put motion sensors around the camp so if he is alive, he can't sneak up on us. It will mean the glyptodon will wake me up fifty times a night, but that's all right.'

Yah had no idea what I'd just said, but he didn't poke at the screen like he usually did. Instead, he made signs with his hands and started chanting something. I hoped it was a protective charm.

Chapter Sixteen

In fact, the smilodon was very much on my mind. I'd put off examining Brett's remains, but I ran out of excuses. Jake was recovering, although still bedridden. Yah had pretty much moved into the campsite – and I think he believed the medbot was alive, because he'd call it, crouching down and patting the ground when he saw it. Or he'd follow it around when it moved. He talked to it, and I got the idea of recording as much as I could of his language.

When I decided to start the report on Brett, it had already been three days since the smilodon had killed him. I recovered the dissolving capsule from his thigh – the smilodon hadn't eaten it. What interested me the most was trying to find out how the smilodon used its canines to kill and if they hampered it eating, but what I found was that like lions, the smilodon used its tongue, which was as rough as a file, to scrape flesh from bone. Otherwise, the animal had most likely been distracted or too disturbed to finish its meal. I recorded everything, used the medbot to help take samples and measurements, then dug a deep pit near Donnell's burial cairn and put Brett's remains in it. I covered him and piled rocks over the grave to keep scavengers out, then I said a little prayer.

'Dear Great Spirit of this era, take this man's soul and set it free. He was a greedy man, he would have killed me without a qualm, but all that is over now. I forgive him. Let him rest in peace. And Donnell too. And Captain Hackab, and Santiago de los Réos as well. As long as we're being magnanimous.'

I leaned on my shovel, and wondered if Yah, who'd gone to the river to fish, had caught anything. He usually went fishing around this time of day, either in one of the shallow creeks feeding the river, or from a rockfall not far from his cave entrance. I knew, because I sent my vidcam after him when he left in order to keep an eye on him. I liked him, and didn't want anything to happen to him, at least not while I was around. Once I'd left, he'd be on his own.

I counted the days. The tractor beam would come back for us in three more days. I had three days to finish getting as many samples of blood as I could, finish filming the smilodon, and pack everything away. Packing would be the most troublesome thing, because Jake would not be able to help me. He could barely sit up. The medbot kept scuttling in to check on him; and most of the time it ended up giving him something to put him to sleep. He was still anaemic and very weak.

'Robin?' My comlink pinged.

Speak of the ghost in your head. 'I'll be right there.' I spoke into my comlink and, putting my shovel on my shoulder, started up the hill. The sun was shining, the sky was blue, and the breeze felt wonderful — balmy and soft as a dandelion puff. There were no dandelions here. They wouldn't reach North America for roughly another ten thousand years. But there were milkweed pods, and their soft silk was greatly prized for insulation and pillow stuffing. The fibre from their stems was used to make rope. I'd seen Yah pick milkweed and strip the fibres from the stems, twining the filaments around his hand into a sort of ball to be dried and braided later. Yah used cattails, milkweed, sinews, and even hair for making ropes. He used cord to tie his clothes on, to tie his hair back, and to make fishing nets and lines. Plant fibres were also used for mats, baskets, bags, and rugs. Several mats had been woven with different colours, forming intricate patterns.

Another handy thing he used was a grinding stone. This was a smooth, bowl-shaped rock that he used to grind grass seeds, nuts, and even tough meat, in order to make it easier to chew. He had a piece of a deer antler that he used as a pestle. He also had a sharpened rock that he used as an axe, a round, fist-shaped rock to crack bones, and narrow slivers of rock to extract marrow. He made arrowheads,

143

spearheads, and basic tools with rocks – and part of his hearth in his cave had been made of clay, although I didn't find any jars or bowls.

In many ways he was far more advanced than I'd imagined. But in other ways, he needed to make some progress. It bothered me that he never washed his eating utensils, and I'd started nagging him about washing his hands and brushing his teeth. Otherwise he was very clean, bathing in the river once or twice a day, and rinsing his leggings and tunics. The leather that his clothing was made of was very soft and supple. It had been scraped clean with stone tools and soaked in water infused with plants containing tannins. Other pieces of leather had been oiled and smoked. Yah's clothing had been sewn together using a bone needle and either animal or plant fibres. They were decorated with quills from porcupines. In his cave, I'd found neat piles of clothing meant for cooler weather. And he even had rain gear made of supple leather rubbed with fatty oil to make it waterproof.

Yah had accompanied me to his cave, but I think the sight of the pile of ashes that was all that was left of the funeral pyre for his wife and children was too much for him because he left soon after we arrived. I hadn't wanted to offend him, but he didn't seem to mind that I stayed behind and examined all his belongings. He went to his cave to fetch things he needed, but he'd mostly made himself comfortable in Santiago's tent.

I walked into my tent and sat at the foot of Jake's bed. He looked at my dirt-stained hands and sweaty face and said, 'You buried him?'

'I thought it best.'

'And when will you think it best to tell me about Captain Hackab and Santiago? Didn't you think I'd worry and try to contact them?' He held up his arm, where his comlink glowed faintly blue. 'No answers.'

'I'll tell you when I think you feel strong enough,' I said, checking his vitals with his vitapak.

'Robin, I'm strong enough. I promise. I also want you to tell me about that little chap who keeps following the medbot around.'

'Oh, that's Yah. I told you about him already. But you keep forgetting because you're drugged out of your mind on pain meds.'

He glowered at me. 'I do remember. But what is he still doing here? He should not be in the base camp.'

I was relieved to see Jake's vitapak glowing green for the first time since he'd been taken ill. 'How would you like to go sit outside? You've been cooped up in the tent for three days. Here, sit up. Let me help you.' I pulled him to his feet and let him lean on me as he shuffled out the tent flap and lowered himself to sit on a rock, facing the river.

'What a beautiful view,' he said.

I pointed to a bird sailing in the sky. 'That's an *Aiolornis incredibilis*. I think you'd call it a giant condor. I sent a vidcam over to film it. Want to see it on the floating screen?' I called up my screen and showed Jake the huge bird as it sailed through air on the thermals, looking for carrion to eat. 'Five-metre wingspan, standing on the ground, it would reach my shoulders.'

Jake nodded. 'Impressive.'

'And there's Yah, fishing. He's standing on the rockslide down below us', I said. 'Look on the floating screen.' I tapped my comlink and activated another vidcam.

'How many vidcams do you have out there?' Jake asked.

'Four. One for the condor, one for Yah, one for the smilodon, and one to keep track of the wolves.'

His face lit up. 'Show me the smilodon!'

I switched vidcams and showed him the smilodon, asleep in his den. 'He comes out in the evening. I haven't gotten a good film of him yet. He's been hunting away from us and out of range. And as for the wolves, they're not close enough to film either – but I have a vid-cam set up on the ridge overlooking the valley they inhabit, so if they come, I hope to see them. They may not come over the ridge though,' I said, anticipating Jake's question. 'They may come along the river bank and head across the swamp. I still have a couple more vidcams I can set up. I just didn't want to leave you alone. I've been staying close by. Just in case.'

Jake enlarged the screen showing the smilodon and augmented the luminosity. 'He's incredible. Look at those colours.'

'We didn't know he'd been such a deep orange, or that his spots

145

would look like those of a Cloud Leopard, that he'd have stripes on his face and legs, or that he'd have such thick fur.' I smiled. 'It's like that ancient poem about a tiger.'

'Tell me,' said Jake, his eyes never leaving the great beast.

I clicked my comlink and found the poem I was looking for.

'Tyger Tyger, burning bright,
In the forests of the night;
What immortal hand or eye,
Could frame thy fearful symmetry?
In what distant deeps or skies.
Burnt the fire of thine eyes?
On what wings dare he aspire?
What the hand, dare seize the fire?
And what shoulder, & what art,
Could twist the sinews of thy heart?
And when thy heart began to beat,
What dread hand? & what dread feet?
What the hammer? what the chain,
In what furnace was thy brain?
What the anvil? what dread grasp,
Dare its deadly terrors clasp!
When the stars threw down their spears
And water'd heaven with their tears:
Did he smile his work to see?
Did he who made the Lamb make thee?'[1]

He nodded, then turned to look at me. 'Did he who made the lamb, make thee? I wonder the same thing about you, Robin.'

'I don't think I can compare with the sabre-toothed tiger,' I said, a stab of hurt surprising me.

'Now that you've avoided talking about it, tell me what happened to the rest of the team, Robin.'

[1] 'The Tyger' from *Songs of Experience* (1794) by William Blake.

I shivered at the tone of his voice. 'Let me show you what I dug out of my leg,' I said. I took Donnell's capsule and dropped it in Jake's hand. 'Check the name.'

He looked at it, frowned, and said, 'I don't understand.'

'Donnell had *my* capsule in his thigh. And about fifteen minutes after we arrived here, my capsule set off a reaction and he dissolved. When I saw that, I panicked, and thinking the capsules were defective, I took mine out. That's when I saw they'd been switched. But they hadn't been switched on purpose. Believe me. *I* was the one who was supposed to die.'

'But . . . why?'

'I was supposed to die, and Donnell would set off the red alert. And Captain Hackab, Brett, and Santiago were going to come and "rescue" him. I don't know what he would have claimed happened to me – probably that I'd been attacked by wolves. It makes a great excuse, doesn't it?'

Jake shook his head slowly. 'What were they doing? Why?'

'Money. Huge profits. More than you can imagine. They came here before, Jake. They were here a hundred years ago and they infected all the animals they could in the area with a disease that Brett made – a man-made typhus that resists our modern antibiotics and is nearly a hundred per cent fatal. They wanted to infect animals here and wait a few generations, then come back, get their antibodies, and go back as heroes to save the world.'

Jake put his face in his hands. 'I can't conceive of such a thing. Whose idea was it?'

'I think it was Santiago's and Brett's. They knew each other, Brett used to go to Mars – and so did Santiago. They must have met and planned everything. Donnell was in on it. And Captain Hackab. What worries me is not knowing who else is part of the plot. Santiago said there were only him and Hackab left – he thanked me for getting rid of Brett and Donnell. But I'm not sure I trust him.'

'What did you do to Brett, Santiago, and Captain Hackab?' Jake asked.

147

'I didn't kill them, Jake. A smilodon attacked Brett, and Captain Hackab and Santiago were eaten by wolves.'

'Is that your story?'

'That's the truth,' I said. 'At least, as far as I know it. I saw the wolves attack Hackab. I didn't actually see Santiago get killed, but the fact that he hasn't come back to the base camp, and I can't find him on my vidcam, seems to indicate he's dead.'

'So, who has the antibodies? You?'

I nodded. 'In fact, Yah does. He's just donating them to me in exchange for chocolate and some insta-meals. He loves the tasteless mush. I haven't been able to fully explain what I'm doing with his blood, and I feel guilty about taking it without his informed consent. I need to get a dire wolf too – tomorrow Yah and I are going to go try to trap one. I also have to make sure Santiago is really dead. I don't want him sneaking back here one night.'

'Do you think he could have survived?'

'Anything is possible. He had body armour, he had his weapons, his backpack was full of food, and I'm sure he could easily survive. He won't be able to move for a while. But I wouldn't put it past him to crawl to a place where he could recover.'

Jake shuddered. 'Take all the vidcams and send them out to look for Santiago. What you said, about him crawling. You don't know him. He'd – he'd kill his own mother if he thought he could get away with it. He's a psychopath.'

'Stop exaggerating,' I said, soothing him.

'No, Robin. You aren't listening to me. I didn't know Santiago before this trip, but I've heard stories. And when my father found out he was coming with us – coming with the rescue squad – he nearly had a fit. But it was too late to change anything. And Santiago financed the whole thing.'

'You could have told me before,' I said. Then another thought struck me. 'You let me go out with him on my own!'

'I knew you'd be all right, Robin,' he said.

I looked at the dot in the sky that was a five-metre bird capable of killing a dire wolf. All the things I wanted to say jumbled in my head. Finally I decided against saying anything. For once I think I made the right decision.

That evening I took night-vision goggles and a high-powered Maha rifle I'd found in Captain Hackab's tent, and I set off into the forest. I wouldn't let Yah follow me, putting the safety perimeter in action as I stepped out and motioning for him to stay with Jake.

Yah was not happy, he complained and gesticulated, but I turned my back on him and headed down the hill, my floating screen in front of me, the five vidcams each projecting images on different parts of the screen.

I moved slowly and silently through the forest. It was eerie at night. The vidcams were set to move in a grid, scanning every centimetre of the area. I thought that if Santiago were still alive, he'd keep to the burnt part of the forest – hardly any underbrush. If he had a sophisticated vitapak, he could still be alive. He could even be mobile. I had to make sure. My plan had been to canvas the forest, then head back along the swamp. The smilodon had gone hunting, he wasn't in his cave, but one of my vidcams picked up his trace. He was on the opposite side of the ravine from me, down near the riverbank, and I wondered if he had spotted the giant beaver. I made sure the vidcam kept following him and checked the other four.

After three hours, I came across the carcass of a dire wolf.

It had been shot with a Maha rifle. I edged closer, but not too close, keeping hidden. If any other wolves had been around, they had left. There was no trace of Santiago. The ground was hard packed and dusty – the wind and the dry leaves combined to erase any tracks he might have left.

I marked the location on my vidmap to come back and get samples from the wolf, then started to leave when I heard a small sound. It seemed to come from the dead wolf. I froze, then, when the sound came again, I left my hiding place and crept towards the noise. The dead wolf seemed to move, and I nearly ran away, but then I saw there was another wolf – a very young one, huddled next to its

149

mother's body. The dead dire wolf had been a lactating female, and this was her unweaned pup.

The pup cringed when it saw me approach, but it was too small and weak to run. I picked it up and held it at arm's length. It weighed practically nothing and was too far gone to even snarl or struggle. The poor thing would probably be dead when I got back to camp, but even dead, it would be a precious source of antibodies.

I was about to stuff it into my backpack, when it whined and licked my hand. I could feel its tiny heart pounding against its ribs. Its fur was soft, but matted where it had soiled itself. Its eyes were blue-grey and sunken in its head. It trembled violently and was severely dehydrated. It was not going to live. It looked at me, its ears flat against its head in fear, and whined softly again. Sighing, I set it down, unclipped my vitapak from my belt, and hooked it up to the dire wolf pup. Then I put the pup and vitapak carefully in my back-pack, and headed back to the base camp. If I hurried, I'd be back before dawn.

The sky was turning grey around the edges when I started up the hill to the campsite. I don't know what made me hesitate. Maybe it was a movement or noise from the dire wolf pup in my backpack. I was half looking out for the glyptodon, my floating screen was just a palm-sized square with a red dot showing where the smilodon had gone (it was too far away to be a threat, although he was moving back towards the ridge and I wondered if he'd caught scent of the dead wolf). He seemed to be heading towards it.

A splash came from the river, and I caught sight of the beaver's sleek back as he swam downstream. In a minute, he vanished behind the base of the hill. That's when I turned my head to see if the dire wolf pup was still alive, and a simultaneous blast of air a loud 'crack' made me drop to the ground and roll. I tossed my pack with the pup into a thick clump of sedge grass, and I kept rolling while trying to figure out where the blast had come from. I recognized it: someone – Santiago, I thought – had fired a Maha gun at me.

Since I didn't know where to go, I kept rolling downhill, looking

150

for cover. Another blast kicked up a stinging, blinding cloud of earth next to my head and I gasped. My night-vision goggles were suddenly covered in dirt and useless, so I tore them off. Blinded by the darkness, I rolled some more. Another shot rang out, and this time I felt the heat of the blast as well as a blow and a searing burn along my back. For an instant I gasped in pain, but panic cleared my head. Desperate for cover, I did what I thought my attacker wouldn't anticipate. I jumped to my feet and sprang in the direction of the pile of boulders at the river's edge. Another blast, and the dirt where my feet had been exploded. I dove behind a boulder, and the boulder swung around, bleating peevishly.

The glyptodon! I dodged its swinging tail and sprinted for another boulder. The glyptodon recognized me and trotted after me, tossing its heavily armoured head up and down. 'Go away!' I cried, swatting at it. But it was too late. A loud report, a thud, and the glyptodon staggered. Its hind legs crumpled under it, and it fell to the side as it tried to pull itself forward. It raised its head and bugled its confusion and hurt.

I crouched behind a nearby rock and unslung my Maha rifle from my back. The gun had been hit and the canon was burnt and useless. I gaped at the twisted metal. Part of me raged, the other part realized the gun had probably saved my life. Then I heard a familiar voice.

'Put your gun down or I kill Jake. Come out from behind that rock, Robin Johnson, and put your hands on your head.'

I hesitated then heard an anguished cry. *Jake!* I eased out from behind the rock. The sun had just risen behind me over the giant spruce forest. The sky was streaked with pearl pink and blue. Ahead of me, the sky was still dark and spangled with stars. Since the light was at my back, I could see ahead of me, and halfway up the hill, near Donnell's and Brett's cairn, stood Santiago, holding Jake in a choke-hold. That wouldn't have stopped Jake, but the gun pressed to his head was more problematic.

I made a show of tossing my gun aside and put my hands over my head, moving purposely straight towards Santiago. With the rising sun shining in his eyes, it would be harder to see me – or at least harder to judge how fast I was moving. At least I hoped that was the case.

'Stop right there,' he said.

I stopped, and tried not to hear the glyptodon as it agonized. Its cries were heart-rending, and very loud. My floating screen was still next to my head, but it was too small to see where the smilodon was located. It seemed to me the smilodon was close to the meadow, coming up along the side of the swamp. If it had gotten a taste of human flesh and liked it, it wouldn't hesitate to attack again. My flesh prickled. Would it go for the wounded glyptodon? The wee pup in my backpack? Or one of us humans? My mind seemed to work at light speed – all those thoughts streaking through it while I waited for Santiago to make a move.

If he were smart, he'd shoot me now, kill Jake, and pack everything up to catch the tractor beam to our time. I hoped he was greedy. He needed to recoup his losses. Money. That was the key. At least, I hoped so.

'Santiago, we can work something out,' I said. 'We're even now. You tried to kill me, I tried to kill you. We both failed, and now we're stuck with each other. I know why you're here. You need the antibodies to make a vaccine. Whatever you do, don't harm Jake. His body is just getting over the Typhus-77, and he'll be making antibodies soon – but he hasn't any yet. If you kill him, you won't get enough.' That was true. Well, somewhat true. I hoped Santiago hadn't studied medicine.

'You're right. I need the antibodies, and you will get them for me. If you do, I won't kill Jake. And if you behave and do exactly as I say, I'll leave you both here when I go back to my time. I'll tell everyone you died. I'll even tell Jake's father he was a hero and died trying to save you. You get me my antibodies, you don't make any trouble, and I don't kill you. That's my deal. Take it or leave it.'

'I accept,' I said without hesitating. 'But you'll leave us supplies, won't you?' I put a tremor in my voice.

Santiago lowered his gun but didn't let go of Jake. 'If I get my antibodies,' he said. 'Now, get up here.'

Jake didn't struggle. He sagged, as if fainting from lack of oxygen, and Santiago shifted to pull him up again. At that moment, Jake twisted violently around, reached behind his shoulder, and grabbed Santiago's gun. Landing on his back, he fired directly into Santiago's chest.

There was a flash, and the sound of the report, but Santiago only staggered. His body armour was still functional. Lazily, he reached down and wrenched the gun from Jake. A week ago, Jake would have been able to best Santiago. A week ago, he wasn't recuperating from a deadly disease that had destroyed most of his red blood cells and left him weaker than the wolf pup. Santiago lifted the gun, aimed, and shot him in the knee.

Jake screamed.

'Nothing can penetrate this armour,' snarled Santiago. To me, he said, 'Your pathetic attempt to hamstring me would have worked if I hadn't had my vitapak with me. But as you can see, I'm invincible.'

At that moment, a shadow appeared behind Santiago and Jake. It moved stealthily through the grass, gathered itself, and sprang.

Santiago must have heard something. He whirled around, but didn't raise his gun. He didn't even try. Perhaps his confidence in his body armour was such that he misjudged the threat. He may have been showing off. Or he thought that Jake was the object of the attack. After all, Jake was obviously wounded – lying on the ground, screaming. But Santiago had forgotten a vital point. True, metal could never penetrate the body amour. Bullets and certain electromagnetic waves were stopped – he could walk through the safety perimeter and suffer no harm. Knives couldn't cut it. Even knives made of atomic ceramics couldn't penetrate. The armour had also been made to withstand wild animal attacks. Keratin makes up claws – and anything with keratin is blocked. Teeth and bone are calcium-based, and the armour could repel those easily. Interesting fact though – matter made of cellulose could go through it – and Yah's spear had a wooden tip.

Yah threw the spear with enough force that it went into Santiago's

153

throat and came out the back of his skull. Santiago gave a sort of hiccough and toppled over, right on top of the pile of stones marking Brett's grave.

I didn't waste time. I snatched my backpack from the sedge grass and sprinted up the hill. Santiago had the best vitapak money could buy. I pawed through his vest, found it, and slapped it on Jake's wrist.

It didn't even need me to tell it what to do. Jake's cries of pain faded as the vitapak dosed him with painkillers.

Yah squatted next to me, an expression of worry on his face. I reached over and patted his shoulder. 'Thank you,' I said.

We got Jake back to the camp and I activated the medbot. It gave Jake a silver cast with turquoise bears on it. Yah was impressed.

The glyptodon was still making a ruckus, and I had an idea. I went back down the hill, carrying the medbot, and set it in the grass next to the poor beast. 'The medbot is our friend,' I said, and I watched as the medbot trotted over and started to explore the glyptodon's injuries. It seemed it had a broken leg. The medbot tranquillized the glyptodon (after a few trials and errors – it had never had to operate on such a beast), removed the bullet, repaired the damage, set the broken bone with pins, and created a cast with green and yellow stars on a chartreuse background.

'Those are horrible colours,' I said, and I laughed as the glyptodon woke, staggered to its feet, and hobbled away, its tail swishing angrily.

I checked my floating screen. The smilodon was now at the edge of the forest, moving towards the river. If I hurried, I could get some samples from it.

Yah helped me track the animal. I used tranquillizer darts to put it to sleep, and collected all the blood I needed. The smilodon fascinated me. I measured its huge canine teeth, drew blood, and stroked its fur. Yah was fearful and incredulous at first, then decided that if I could do it, so could he. He marched over to the smilodon and squatted next to its head, then reached out and tweaked a whisker and jumped back. The huge feline didn't twitch. Yah frowned, poked it, and then pressed his hand to the animal's chest, feeling the rise and fall of its ribs as it breathed. He lifted one of the paws – it was so heavy he needed both hands – and examined the claws, then he twisted and looked at the old scar on his shoulder.

All his life, he'd been terrified of smilodons. He'd most likely been attacked by one when he was younger. And now he was – I tried not to laugh – sitting on the creature's back, leaning over to get a good look at its teeth.

'All right, Yah. That's enough. We have to go now. I don't think you want to be sitting there when he wakes up, so come on.' I mimed the cat yawning and getting to his feet, and Yah scrambled off its back and picked up his spear.

We went a safe distance away and waited. We watched as the smilodon shook its head, got to its feet, and then stretched. After a moment it lifted its head and sniffed the air. We held our breath, tense, ready to run if necessary. But the smilodon just turned and headed back towards the heart of the forest.

We spent the last three days processing the samples. The wolf pup was still alive when I got it back to camp, and it seemed to be thriving with the medbot's care. And with Yah's care. When it could walk again, it followed Yah everywhere. At first Yah had been wary, watching the pup with trepidation. But soon he was feeding him scraps, picking him up and hugging him when he cried, and even letting the pup sleep at the foot of his bed.

Jake made good progress too – and he and Yah spent a lot of time together going to film the various animals they spotted with the vidcams. The film library was full, and the museum's directors would be happy.

But I wasn't happy, and Yah was upset. We had to leave. Yah watched us pack everything, a frown on his face. I'd tried to explain, but how to tell him we were going, and would never come back? How to explain the twelve thousand years that separated us from his time? All I could do was to leave him my entire supply of chocolate, telling him not to give it to the wolf, because it would make him sick. And not to eat it all in one day.

155

Jake was still weak, but he helped me the best he could. I piled everything near the pickup point. We'd toss it in the beam before stepping in ourselves. Then we'd be surrounded by the electrical membrane. We'd be able to see out, for a while at least. Then we'd start to tingle, vibrate, and pass out as the beam froze us and started to unravel our DNA. It would take an hour from the time the beam appeared to the time we were sucked back to our time. Because basically, it was just like a giant, magnetic straw that would break us apart and turn us into stardust. Then we'd arrive and the process would reverse itself, and we'd wake up, be sick, have throbbing headaches and be sick some more. I wasn't looking forward to the trip home.

I was even more reluctant because when I got back, I'd be arrested immediately.

Hopefully Jake's father had found me a good lawyer.

PART III

SHYLOCK:

Most learnèd judge, a sentence! Come prepare!

PORTIA:

Tarry a little, there is something else.
This bond doth give thee here no jot of blood;
The words expressly are 'a pound of flesh'.

Shakespeare, *The Merchant Of Venice,*
Act 4, Scene 1, 304–307

Chapter Seventeen

'Robin Johnson, you are under arrest. You have the right to remain silent. Your attorney will be in shortly to see you. Please stop struggling. You'll only hurt yourself.'

My head hurt. And for some reason, so did my arms. I blinked. My arms were chained to the sides of a bed. My comlink was missing from my wrist. A large floating screen blocked the face of the person speaking to me. I blinked again, harder, trying to clear my vision. This wasn't the cold white sending room. I wasn't lying on the slab of quartz, shivering and retching. Had that already happened? I searched my memory but found nothing. Everything seemed vague, like a dream. 'Where am I?'

'You're in the prison hospital in Anchorage. Did you understand what I said to you before? You are under arrest, you have the right—'

'I heard you. I understand. What am I accused of?' As if I didn't know. A weight seemed to settle on my chest.

'Murder.' The word echoed weirdly around the windowless room.

'I'd like my comlink, please.'

'Denied.'

'Who are you?' I craned my neck, but a knock sounded at the door, and I never got an answer. The man left. My lawyer entered. There was a nanosecond I thought – no it wasn't who I'd thought. Was it? It was! Suddenly I couldn't see, I couldn't breathe. I tried to speak, but only sobs came out.

'I'm sorry, Robin. I should have come sooner. I should have

contacted you. I'm sorry. But I'm here now.' She sat down and put her hand on my shoulder, pressing gently. 'Yasmine would have wanted me to represent you. When I heard from Dr Powell, I didn't hesitate an instant. I want you to know that, Robin.'

'It's all right. It's just that you look so much like her. So very much.' I closed my eyes. Tears ran down my cheeks. I felt my nose running too, and that stopped my crying. 'I can't wipe my face. The *wang bas* tied me down.'

She took a soft facecloth from the distributor on the wall, came back and cleaned my face. 'Better?'

'Thank you, Sing.'

'You're welcome.'

'So, you're my lawyer?'

'I'm your attorney. It's even better.' She sat next to me, her hands clasped in her lap. Then she looked at me and said, 'Yasmine told me you made holos of her.'

'If you want, I'll show them to you.'

Sing smiled sadly. 'I'd like that. I miss her so much,' she said. 'When I see you, I see her. I see you two giggling. I never thought it was important to giggle with someone until I saw you and Yasmine. You were always laughing together.'

'I miss her too. I –' I nearly said I missed the whole family, but didn't.

She knew though. She bowed her head. 'We didn't mean to push you away, Robin. Our grief made us selfish. We only thought of ourselves. I tried to use my work as a way to forget. I took a job on Mars – anything to get away. Li Wei and Bolin came with me. Chenric decided to take a break and has been in Tibet. Wait. I know. Just a moment.' She fussed with her comlink and called a floating screen. Soon there were three people on it. Li Wei and Bolin, Yasmine's two brothers, were still on Mars. Yasmine's father, Chenric, stood in front of an ancient temple.

'Greetings, everyone,' I said. I grinned. 'I'd love to wave, but as you can see . . .' I raised my wrists as far as I could.

'May the sun and stars shine blessings upon you, Robin.' Chenric

160

bowed and then smiled. 'I'm joyful to see you. Even in these circumstances. I'm sure Sing will prevail and you will soon be free.'

'Thank you, Chenric, it's good to see you too. Boys, I hope you're behaving yourselves in your mother's absence,' I said. I looked at Sing. 'Is anyone listening on this screen?'

'No, it's secure,' she said.

'Boys – (Yasmine had always called her twin brothers boys – she said she couldn't tell them apart) what is the news about the Typhus-77? Are the immigrants going to be allowed to come to Mars?'

Bolin shook his head. (For some reason, *I* could tell them apart). 'No, the Mars Corp has refused to let them in. We heard via newscasts that you and Jake managed to bring back enough antibodies to develop vaccines, but rumour has it that the immigrants are already sick. And another rumour says that the vaccine will never make it to Mars. The Western State of California has claimed it and will defend it with military power if necessary. Mars isn't interested in starting a war, so it has simply shut down its immigration programme. If we leave, we may not be able to come back.'

'Will the vaccine be shared at all?' I asked.

'It's being shared with New England to protect the herds of bison and caribou. Eurasia will get some as well for the great plains in the north, to save their yak and camels. China is negotiating, but since Typhus-77 is only in the northern hemisphere, it hasn't been affected yet. The Kingdom of Brazil is also interested.'

'And the Still United States of the South?' I asked.

The boys shook their heads. 'No.' Li Wei, as concise as ever.

Bolin added, 'They haven't asked. They demanded their share. They say that since Donnell was born there, his part of the vaccines must belong to the South. They've sent armed—'

Sing interrupted. 'That's enough. We should not discuss the matter. Stay on Mars for now, boys, and Chenric, if you could find it in your heart to return, I would be most grateful.'

Chenric bowed again. 'It will be as my wife demands. Robin, I look forward to seeing you. Be calm, my little fury. Sing will take care of you.'

161

I smiled, despite the pain in my chest. I'd not forgotten how formal Chenric was, and it touched me to hear his nickname for me – Little Fury. 'I'm looking forward to seeing you too. But before you go, I need to know what that poem was that you sent me after Yasmine . . .' my voice trailed off. I couldn't even bring myself to admit she was gone. 'It went, *"Nothing is sadder than the last snowflake in spring. Nothing says desolation like the last leaf in autumn whirling through the wind. And yet we long for the first snowfall, and we treasure the first green leaf"*.'

Yasmine's father smiled. 'It was just something I wrote when I was very young and not a very good poet, I'm afraid.'

'It kept me busy thinking of what you meant and took my mind off things,' I said.

'If that's true, then it served its purpose.' Chenric bowed.

Sing made a graceful, waving motion with her hand and shut off the screen. She'd recovered her poise, and I recognized the professional taking over. 'You don't have to tell me anything,' she said. 'We can work out a defence that will enable you to remain silent. No one can make you—'

'Sing, I did not kill anyone. I swear. I swear on the memory of your daughter that I did not kill Donnell, or Brett, or Captain Hackab, or Santiago.'

She looked disconcerted for the first time. 'Then, how did they die?'

'Donnell had my dissolving capsule in his thigh. Somehow they must have gotten switched.'

'Do you swear under oath that this is the truth?'

'I swear.'

'Hold on. Wait.' She switched a screen back on, reached in her purse, and took out a tiny vidcam. It was the size and shape of a green dragonfly. It left her hand and hovered in the air in front of me. 'This is the deposition of Robin Johnson. The date is thirty-first January, 3378. Robin has agreed, under oath, to tell the truth about her trip to the Palaeolithic era, a voyage which cost the life of four men. Robin, you may tell your story now.'

I looked at the little dragonfly vidcam and began. 'If I'm to tell everything about the trip back to time and its aftermath – the reason for the voyage, why I was chosen for the trip, and who got killed – I have to start at the beginning. As my boss, Dr Powell, would say: "You have to know the background of anything before you can put it into context." He was also fond of saying, "If you precipitate matters you will not be precise." That's a good saying – and one that I always remember, mostly because Dr Powell said it nearly every day. I will therefore take my time and explain everything fully.'

Three hours later, when I'd finished telling the story, Sing stood and stretched her back and arms. 'I will ask that you be remanded to Dr Powell's custody until and for the duration of the trial, which won't happen until July. We have six months to plan our defence. There are several plaintiffs: the families of the men who died, and also the Still United States of the South is bringing charges, although not necessarily against you. They just want Donnell's part of the vaccine. But I will be frank – the antibodies belong to you and to Jake. You might want to consult a financial advisor.'

'I will. But it's only fair that everyone gets it. A vaccine is only good as herd protection. If we can't vaccinate everyone, then it's useless. I'm putting the vaccine in the public domain. No one will be able to patent it, and I refuse to profit from it.' I shrugged. 'Sing, can you get someone in here to unchain me? I have to go to the bathroom.'

She nodded. 'I'm going to get you out of here. Maybe not today, or even tomorrow, but by the end of the week you will be with Dr Powell and his wife. They insisted.'

The relief I felt nearly undid me. Some part of me managed to hold on, and when the guard came, I was dry-eyed and calm. I was still calm when he led me back, and this time there were no chains; I was free to move around the room. Sing had even managed to get a comfortable chair and desk moved in, and a floating screen. I couldn't control the screen – it showed me a generic news channel. My comlink was still confiscated, and I couldn't call or receive calls, except from my attorney.

163

I sat next to the wall, put my hand over a crack in the shiny paint, and whispered, 'What doesn't kill me, better run fast.'

A soft voice sounded in my head. It had started with the medbot song. Mothers sing that to their children so they're not afraid when they see the medbot. Now, small things started to come back, surges of memory, nothing clear yet, but all of it strong and getting stronger. I drew my knees to my chest and wrapped my arms around them.

Memories were overlapping like waves, moving like the tide, floating closer and closer. I closed my eyes and breathed deeply. In the psychiatric ward, where I'd spent most of my youth, there had been one doctor who was convinced I suffered from survivor's guilt. She'd even published a paper on my case, but despite all her efforts had made no headway helping me remember. But she was one of the few who never doubted. She'd tell me over and over, '*Robin, it's likely you will never remember what happened, but that's not important. Have confidence in yourself. That's what I want you to learn. That, and how to trust.*'

I dug my fingernails into the crack and peeled off a sliver of paint. I had seen holos and stills of my parents. They had been scientists. That was in the newsreels, the holos, and I knew their story by heart. My father worked in a secret program at Tempus U. That was nothing odd – there were hundreds of secret programs there. My mother was a mathematician and had helped develop an algorithm program that analysed current events. The program was still being used. My mother had wanted to go a step further, to develop a program that would actually *predict* changes instead of just *observing* them, but her work had been interrupted when she'd died.

My father had been brilliant as well – but something had happened. No one ever found out why he came home one night, killed my mother, then killed himself. He left no note, there was no sign, at least, nothing to explain his actions. I was there. I saw it all, but mercifully, I couldn't remember, and I'll never know why he did it. Sometimes, my doctors told me, we can never understand. Some people act without reason. My father may have had a psychotic incident, he may have had a brain tumour, he may have been in a severe depression. All I could do is learn to live with it. And that's what I finally did. I never would understand why it happened, but when I finally stopped feeling guilty, when I finally stopped looking for answers, that's when the doctors told me I was cured. They asked me to trust myself, then, perhaps if I was one of the lucky ones, I'd learn to trust others. I'd started by trusting Yasmine, then I'd trusted Dr Powell, and now I trusted Sing to clear my name.

Chapter Eighteen

After I gave my deposition, things moved quickly. Sing got my trial moved forward. I left the hospital and was confined to Dr Powell's house. Mrs Powell fussed over me, which I was pretty sure I hated, even though I could get used to having a cup of hot chai and home-made dumplings brought to me on a tray every morning.

'You saved Jake's life,' she said to me, and hugged me for the hundredth time.

Dr Powell just wanted to know when I'd be coming back to work. 'It's not like we don't have things to do,' he said, bringing me a stack of holodisks to scan. 'Try to finish this by tomorrow. The museum wants you to go report to them. They're still sorting through the films you and Jake brought back. Not bad. Not bad at all.' He hesitated, then said, 'You know, I understand what you did. But . . .' his voice trailed off.

'We talked about this.' I frowned. 'I did it because I know you'll do what's right with the vaccines.'

'I'm going to do my best.' He cleared his throat. 'You realize you've destroyed my retirement plans completely.'

I had to wait nearly a week before Jake came to see me. He was so thin his wrist bones stuck out, he walked with a limp, and when I saw him I burst into tears but pretended it was just anxiety about my trial. 'It's nothing. Don't worry. Sing is taking great care of me. What about you? How do you feel?' I asked, hugging him and wincing at the feel of his ribs.

'Fine. Tired. They keep draining my blood. I feel like I'm

166

surrounded by vampires.' He shook his head. 'I would have been to visit sooner but they kept me in the med-centre. My closest friend is my medbot right now. And . . .' his voice trailed away. 'Helen wants to announce our wedding. I wanted to be the first to tell you.'

'Oh. Well, congratulations.' I let go of him, stepped back, and gave him a crooked grin. 'She finally wore you down.' Red spots appeared on his cheeks. Apparently, I still hadn't learned how to respond correctly to a wedding announcement. 'Sorry. Forget that last phrase. Just congratulations.'

He rubbed his forehead. 'I have a bunch of contracts for us to sign. Did you get them?'

I had. They were all about the antibodies. Yah's belonged to me, as did the ones I'd gotten from the fauna. But Jake's were his, and I'd agreed to share profits from the samples I'd taken from the wolves and the smilodon. Since I didn't want any money, and I felt the vaccine belonged to everyone on Earth, the Moon, and Mars, I'd taken my whole lot and transferred the rights to the only person I had confidence in: Jake's father. 'Did your dad say anything?' I asked, uncertainly.

'About the wedding? He said, "About time." That's all.' Jake cocked his head. 'That isn't what you meant though, is it? Why did you give him your shares? What are you planning to do after the trial?'

'You heard that the Mars Corp is putting a cap on the number of immigrants,' I said. 'There will be many who won't be able to go. They can't stay here. There isn't enough food for everyone. Our resources are limited. They can't go south. They can't go east. New England is in worse shape than we are; so is Eurasia. Africa won't be habitable for decades.' I shook my head. 'The Kingdom of Brazil won't take anyone.'

'What are you saying?' Jake sat next to me on the couch. 'The ones that are left will be given a choice. The strongest ones will be sent to Africa to help with the clean-up, but the younger ones might be able to negotiate with the Mars Corp.'

'Yes,' I said bitterly. 'Sell their labour in exchange for a trip to Mars. Asteroid mining for the rest of their lives. It's slavery, Jake. And Africa is a death sentence. Euthanasia would be kinder.'

'What do you expect us to do?' Jake said angrily. 'We can't feed everyone, you know that. We can keep them alive, but they'll have to make hard choices. If you want them to die, then don't give up your shares of the vaccine for free. Let the Typhus-77 decide who lives or who dies. Is *that* what you want?'

'No,' I said. I took his hand, then dropped it. The touch of his skin made my own skin tingle. 'No. I want to take everyone who wants to go with me back in time. We're going to resettle the area that Santiago and Brett decimated. By their fault, Yah lost his family. Countless lives were lost. No one knows where the native North and South American natives first came from. Well, they came from now.'

Jake froze. 'Are you serious?' he asked, finally.

'Yes. And if you're wondering, I've already talked about this with your parents, with Sing, and with the director of Tempus U. Everyone thinks it's a good idea. Especially Sing. She says the Carlysle family is not going to accept my getting off free after Santiago died. They're going to make my life hell.'

'But, Robin, what am I going to do without you?' Jake sounded truly distraught.

'You're going to get married and have one point two children. What do you want me to say, Jake? That I'm going to miss you? Of course I will.' I stopped and shook my head. 'But we both know it's better like this. For everyone.'

My trial was moved up for two reasons. My idea of going back to the Palaeolithic had met with support from all sides. Even the Mars Corp was willing to drop charges against me and let bygones be bygones – as long as I took the leftover immigrants with me. Another reason was the testimony from Santiago's uncle, Edward Carlysle, who, posing as one of the more decent Carlysles, told everyone that he'd long suspected Santiago of wrongdoing.

The first part of the trial was for Donnell's death. There, we heard Dr Grace Feldman, who explained how the capsules had been mixed up. It was also the first time I heard myself referred to as a sociopath, which I thought had been expunged from my records after my release from the asylum. However, as I learned then, not only does it stay, but it's accessible to anyone with a comlink. No wonder I couldn't get a date for my uni ball.

> **Dr Feldman:** '*Of course I didn't tamper with the capsules. But I wondered why Donnell Urbano came to the lab the day before the trip. If you want, you can have copies of the security tapes. We didn't think to verify them. If he reset the timer on Ms Johnson's capsule, it backfired spectacularly. If anything it was my fault, because I was distracted by Ms Johnson. Sociopaths can be extremely charming—*'
>
> **Ms Sing Schwartz, defence attorney:** '*Objection! Strike that last comment.*'
>
> **Prosecutor:** '*I object as well.*'
>
> **Judge**: '*Overruled. Keep that statement.*' (*Aside, to his aide*) '*That's the first time both sides objected to the same thing.*'
>
> ~ Excerpt from Dr Grace Feldman's testimony.

After that, we recessed until the next day. Sing reassured me that the trials for Captain Hackab's and Brett's deaths were just formalities. We had no trace of Hackab's body, but we had recordings of his conversations with Brett, Santiago, and Jake, recovered from Brett's comlink. Everything corresponded to my testimony. As for Brett, the holo of his autopsy performed (rather messily) by myself made most of the jury rush out of the room. Dr Powell's remark that I could have been neater went unnoticed in the commotion.

Santiago's death, the last one to happen, was the last one I was tried for. We had brought his body back with us, and his wounds were compared to Jake's and my testimonies. Holos were shown to the jury, the judge, and our legal teams. Then I testified. Sing asked me only about what had happened with Santiago, starting with our meeting and ending with Yah's attack on him. After, Santiago's uncle, Edward Carlysle, was called to testify. I didn't appreciate being called a socio-path by the judge, but since Sing assured me that it wouldn't matter, I kept my thoughts to myself. At least mostly to myself.

1 May, 3378, Anchorage District Court, Edward Carlysle on the stand.

Judge: *'If you knew she was a sociopath, why did you choose her to go back in time?'*

Edward Carlysle: *'Because we knew she'd get the job done.'*

Judge: *'Did you know about the previous trip that Dr Brett Kavanaw, Santiago de los Réos, and Captain Jermaine Hackab had done? And how the Carlysle company was involved?'*

Edward Carlysle: *'The company was never involved. Let me set that record straight. As for the Typhus-77, we suspected, but couldn't prove anything. What we can prove is how Santiago took money from the company to pay for everything. We think we should be compensated.'*

Judge: *'So you're saying you set Robin Johnson up and sent her into danger knowing the risks she would take?'*

Edward Carlysle: *'Well . . .' (sound of throat clearing) 'We never thought she was the one in danger.'*

Judge: *'So you knowingly sent these men to their deaths?'*

Edward Carlysle: *'No, of course not. I mean to say that we hoped that Robin would find out what had happened and would do the right thing.'*

Judge: *'The right thing? You mean, find proof that the Typhus-77 was manmade? That the Carlysle company financed it? That one of its members had knowingly contributed to what amounts to a genocide?'*

Edward Carlysle: *(Hesitates) 'I suppose this means we won't be compensated for the vaccine.'*

Robin Johnson: *(Shouting) 'That's one thing you got right, wang ba!'*

Judge: *(The judge has to bang his gavel and shout to be heard over the din) 'Order! Order, I say! Case dismissed. Robin Johnson, you are free to go.'*

And all I could think was, free to go back twelve thousand years. Twelve thousand years away from Jake.

Chapter Nineteen

They let me take my medbot. I had a list as long as my arm. And nothing would disintegrate. The immigrants 'chosen' to go back with me were the ones no one wanted. So I made sure they knew I wanted them, needed them, and we would do more than just survive.

The films Jake and I made were shown over and over – until everyone was familiar with the bluff, the meadow, the river, the forests, and the mega-fauna that lived there. What made things easier was the fact that many of these people had come from a rural, farming society in what used to be Central America, and most of them knew how to grow crops and build houses. We'd have to fit in with the Palaeolithic societies already in place, so we swapped our modern clothes for leather and woven flax, made sure we all had comlinks that looked like leather bracelets, and had a contest to design the best dwelling. Someone even came up with the idea of how to disguise a medbot as a clay pot. All in all, by the time the spring rains had ceased, we were ready for our new lives.

I'd selected a date not far from when we'd left. There were several reasons for this. I knew the area, the fauna, and I was hoping Yah would still be around. I planned to assimilate him into our group. It wouldn't be easy, but some of the people were linguists, and they'd been studying his tapes, learning some of his words and gestures. Yah was to be our guide. I was also looking forward to seeing my pal the glyptodon. Hopefully his leg had healed.

We would set up a first settlement in the meadow, on the bluff, and along the river. After, we'd start moving. The land would not be able to sustain such a large number of people right away. We would have to develop crops, domesticate animals, and learn how to get by before winter came. We would cheat the first year, with enough food to last, but we couldn't take much with us. For one thing, resources were so low it would mean hunger for people in this time. The sooner we left, the better. And everyone, even the immigrants, or the settlers, as we'd taken to call ourselves, knew it.

An envelope made of real paper landed on my desk. Dr Powell, who was with me that day, looked at it, then left the room. I picked up the envelope. We didn't use paper anymore. I rubbed my fingertips over it, admiring the smooth creamy texture. Someone had written my name on it with real ink. Another rarity. I lifted it to my nose and sniffed the unfamiliar odours. To open it, I'd have to rip the delicate flap on the back. I knew that, but it took a while before I pushed my finger beneath the corner and slid it to the right. Immediately a shooting pain stabbed me, and I pulled my hand back, staring at the papercut on my index. Blood beaded the edge of the cut then trickled down my skin. I'd never had a papercut. I'd read about them – in ancient times people who handled paper got them all the time. I turned my hand to the light, examining the wound, wondering how something so frail could cut so deeply. A drop of blood fell on the envelope and spattered on the paper. With a sigh, I activated my vitapak and it sprayed a little bandage over my cut. Then I took the envelope, ripped it open, and took out the card. It was the invitation to Helen's and Jake's wedding. I checked the date. Sure enough, it was for right after my voyage back in time. At least I wouldn't have to go to *that* ceremony. Part of me was relieved. The other part tore the card into tiny pieces. I took my time. I'd never torn up paper before, and I wanted to enjoy it.

I gave all my holos of Yasmine to Sing. I kept the last one, the one I wasn't supposed to open until I was thirty. I was almost there, just another month to go. I'd open it when I went back in time, when it wouldn't matter how old I was, because I wouldn't be born for another twelve thousand years.

172

The last week I spent in my own time, I managed to avoid a dinner with 'Friends and Family of Helen and Jake', organized by Helen. I could hear the relief in her voice when I said I couldn't make it. I did spend several evenings with Sing and Chenric, and the last evening I gave them the holos and hugged them goodbye. We laughed. We cried. I felt like I was part of a family and was grateful.

The day of my departure, the Time Sender in charge of sending my atoms spinning into the past woke me up at four a.m. to get me ready. My group arrived one by one. Over a period of months, ten to twelve people at a time would go back . Different supplies would arrive with each group. My group had the tent city, the water purifiers, and the basic medical and scientific labs. After that, the farmers, the hunters, the livestock breeders, the builders, and the various experts needed to get everything started would arrive. Season by season, we'd build the new world. In small groups, some would go south, others would head east. It would be difficult, but far better than a life as an asteroid miner. The immigrants had started calling themselves 'Settlers', and the seven people in the room with me were cheerful as they prepped for our voyage.

Seven? I looked around. There should be ten, plus me. Where were the other three people? Had they decided they'd rather take their chances with the Mars Corp after all?

'Where are the others? Aren't there supposed to be ten?' I asked the Time Sender.

He paused, then finished putting the intravenous into my arm. He patted the medbot absently and said to me, 'They're on their way. There was a last-minute change. But don't worry. The team has been approved by Dr Powell.'

'That's good,' I said. And then the beam of light came down, the cold washed over me, and I passed out.

As before, waking up after travelling through time is a dismal experience. Since there were so many of us, plus our supplies, we each woke up encased in our own safety bubble. I can't even imagine how much this was costing Tempus U, but since I gave part of my shares to them as well as to Dr Powell, I figured I'd paid for my team's voyage ten times over.

I lay on the ground and shivered and retched, and waited for my bones to stop aching. When I could, I looked around. The meadow looked the same. I'd asked to be sent back as near as possible to the time I'd last left, but there was no way, so far back, to be precise. It could be a week, a month, or ten years after I'd been here last. There was no sign of the glyptodon in the valley. The river looked the same, but I didn't see the giant beaver. Perhaps he was somewhere else. Perhaps he was long dead. I didn't let myself think about Yah.

I didn't wait until the forcefield subsided. Braving the sting, I put my shoulder into it and rolled out. Standing up, I looked around. From the outside, the bubbles looked like spheres of mist. I was the first to emerge. The supplies were still encased in mist as well. I decided to hike up the bluff and see what was left of the campsite.

I called up my floating screen and scouted the area. I didn't want to meet the dire wolf pack or the smilodon, but there was no sign of either. When I reached the top of the bluff, all that was left of the camp was a rough circle of rocks where the firepit had been.

I knelt and put my hand on the blackened earth. The ashes were cold and damp. I sniffed the air. There was still a faint smell of smoke though. I stood and lifted my head, breathing deeply. It wasn't the smell of old smoke. This was from burning wood. There was a fire nearby. In my mind two images appeared. Yah, and a funeral pyre.

I started to run. I pelted down the hill and found the trail that led around the side of the cliff. The trail followed the river. I ran, stumbled, nearly fell, then ran some more. My feet felt numb. The time-travel fatigue had yet to wear off. Some moments, I could hardly see because of blurred vision, but I kept running. I hit a rock, fell, skinned my hands and knees. But I got up and ran. And I yelled. 'Yah! Yah! Yah!'

At the base of the cliff, where the rough steps were hewed into the rock, I stopped, my chest heaving, and leaned over, my hands on my knees. I gasped for breath, lifted my head and was about to scream, 'Yah!', when a huge dire wolf stepped onto the path.

174

I collapsed. Fear, like jagged bolts of electricity, made my whole body convulse. I'd come all this way, and now I'd die, torn apart by a dire wolf. I moaned softly and shut my eyes. Nothing happened. I opened one eye, then the other. The wolf stood in the path. It cocked its head, then turned. And I saw Yah.

He came down the path and stopped, his eyes widening. He must have been near the river, fishing. Water glistened on his skin.

I pointed to the dire wolf. 'He grew up,' I said, my voice shaking. I managed to get to my feet. The relief I felt nearly crumpled my legs again, but I braced myself. I grinned at him, trying to get my breath. 'Greetings, Yah,' I gasped, finally.

He reached out and poked me. Then he poked me again, and then he started to laugh and cry. He sat down, put his head in his hands, and sobbed. The wolf, unsure, whined. Yah pulled the wolf to him and hugged him. Then he got up and hugged me, and motioned to me to hug the wolf (which I admit, I was afraid to do at first, but the huge beast seemed to like me, and licked my face).

I motioned to Yah, telling him that lots of people were here now, and that more were coming. He'd never be alone again. And I managed to stop shaking. Because when I'd smelled the smoke, the first thing that came to mind was his desolation when we left, and how he'd begged us to stay. I'd been terrified the smoke came from a funeral pyre. I'd panicked when I imagined him standing next to it, ready to throw himself into the fire.

When we'd left, he'd circled the beam of light, crying and trying to reach in. To be alone was terrifying. In this time period, it was as good as a death sentence. But he'd had his dire wolf pup, now nearly fullgrown.

'Come on. Let's go meet the rest,' I said to him, helping him to his feet.

'Robin,' he said, poking me again, and then sighing deeply.

We walked back towards the meadow. In the river, I caught sight of a ripple and a sleek, brown head. The beaver still patrolled his territory. The vegetation hadn't changed much. The dire wolf still looked juvenile. Perhaps just one year had gone by. I'd know soon.

The lab would be set up. We'd be able to tell time. That thought made me laugh, and Yah laughed too.

I was starting to feel better. My head stopped spinning, my vision cleared. As we approached the meadow, I heard my name being called. Others had woken, left their bubbles, and most likely wondered where I'd gone. Yah hesitated when he heard the voices, but I motioned at him to come. 'It's fine, don't worry. They're friends.'

The dire wolf didn't seem aggressive, and when it saw the people, it pricked its ears. Yah scratched its head, and reassured, the dire wolf trotted with us into the meadow, where several people milled around our supplies, sorting things into piles. The people froze when they saw the dire wolf, but I motioned to them to continue what they were doing. 'It's all right!' I said loudly. 'They're friends! The big dog is friendly!'

Yah stopped and tugged my arm. 'Robin! Aki Jake? Aki adeez?' he said urgently.

My heart lurched, but I managed to smile. 'He's fine. Jake adeez is far, far away. He's fine. Really,' I said, seeing his confusion.

Yah let go of me and started running, the wolf loping at his side. I chased after them. 'Yah!' I cried, 'Come back. I'm sorry. I wish he could be here too.'

Yah had stopped in front of someone. He waved his arms and babbled, and the person stepped back, obviously frightened of the huge dire wolf. I hurried over, intending to apologize and to explain. My words died on my lips. Standing in front of me, twelve thousand years after I'd just left him for the last time, was Jake.

'Jake!' said Yah. His grin took up all his face.

'What are you doing here? Is Helen here too? How could you leave? How – how could you do that to your parents?' I hit his chest. 'How could you leave them?'

'Who said I left them?' Jake grabbed my arms and held me still. 'No, Helen isn't here. You know me. Start talking about weddings and I get hives. I don't know how we even got to the invitation stage. I must have been still delirious from the virus.'

'But your parents, Jake. '

'They came too. There were three last-minute changes.'

I looked, and there they were. Dr Powell. Jeannie. Both there, both looking ragged and sick from the trip back in time. They'd recover. I started to laugh, and Jake hugged me.

'I wasn't going to let you go,' he said. 'Not this time. Not ever again.'

A storm moved through the valley, lightning like wobbly legs under a huge, bloated grey body. The spruce trees leaned and cracked, and the sound of breaking branches echoed in the sky as lightning lashed down and a whipcrack of thunder curled across the sky. In the valley, the tents strained against their tethers, but none gave. Rain rolled off the domes, and over to the side, the glyptodon, illuminated by a flash of lightning, lifted its head and eyed its harem.

Yah was in his cave with several of the new settlers. A linguist had started communicating with Yah, building a vocabulary we'd all use. I imagined the cave would be far more cosy in this storm than the tents. The wind would be muted. Some rain might rush in, but the settlers would be gathered around Yah's fire, sitting on soft furs, and drinking hot chocolate. The dire wolf would be lying in its place by the door, staring out at the storm, protective of its new clan.

Up on the bluff, Jake and I sat in our tent and watched the storm. We had hot chocolate. And soft furs. We'd gotten rid of our modern textiles for the trip back in time. And now I put my floating screen on for one of the last times. When our batteries ran out, we'd be hooked up to the small sun-cells we'd brought with us, but mostly we'd be dependent on the wind and water power. Already some settlers had unhooked their technology and firelight flickered in their tents, smoke streaming from makeshift chimneys.

I opened the last holo Yasmine made for me.

'Hey there, Robin.' Yasmine looked transparent, lying on the white sheets, hooked up to the medbots. 'I know you're not thirty yet. That's all right. I wouldn't have waited either. But I'm guessing you chose this day for a reason to see me one last time. Either you're about to jump out of a window, or you finally got rid of that insufferable Helen and got your Jake at last.'

I paused the holo while I choked on my hot chocolate, and Jake pounded my back. 'Sorry about that,' I said.

He pointed at Yasmine. 'I hope she was joking about the window part.'

'Not really,' I said. 'Things were pretty dark for a while.'

'No more bad thoughts,' he said. 'Have some more chocolate.'

'I used to think chocolate was the panacea of life,' I said. I took a sip of my hot chocolate. 'It's good, but it's not as good as having you with me, Jake.'

He kissed my throat, just where my pulse beat, just above my collarbone. 'I know what you mean,' he whispered. 'Now, put the holo back on.'

'So, girl, this is the last holo. You don't need me anymore. And I'm not just saying that. You're the tough one. I was the beautiful one – but you, Robin, were my strength. I never told you how many times I was afraid – afraid to take a test, afraid to talk to someone, or afraid to try something new. I was afraid of death. But then I met you. You might not realize this, but you helped me through the university, through my first heartache, my first failure, and you helped me when I got my first diagnosis, when they told me that what I had was incurable. I kept thinking of you, Robin. You saw death firsthand, and it nearly annihilated you, but you made it back from the other side. Everything you felt was wrong about yourself was what I needed. I needed your candid remarks, your honesty, and your toughness. I needed you to tell my family to stop crying over me. Yeah, my mom told me. And you did right, because if I saw one more tear *I* was going to jump out of the window.' She took a minute to get her breath back. Then she shivered, and said, 'I wish I could be with you, Robin, you know that. We had fun together, we made each other laugh. But now it's time for you to move on. Have a good life. If you want, you can name your first child after me. But only if it's a girl.' She grinned, and the holo ended.

I wiped tears off my cheeks and had another sip of chocolate. And then Jake wrapped his arms around me, and he kissed me again. A crack of lightning lit up the tent, and thunder rumbled overhead. Rain battered the roof.

'It's a dark and stormy night in the Palaeolithic era,' I said, settling back in Jake's arms. 'But I have a feeling tomorrow is going to be a beautiful day.'

Dear Reader

You don't know how excited I am to be welcoming you to Genovia, home of the most not-ready-for-royalty princess ever, Amelia Mignonette Grimaldi Thermopolis Renaldo.

It's been fifteen years since we were allowed our first glimpse into the diaries of Princess Mia (and introduced to Genovia, that glittering little principality tucked along the sea between France and Italy), and so much has happened since then:

We used to shop in stores. Now we shop online. Phones hung on the wall. Now we keep them in our pockets. We used to go to the record store. Now we download music.

But where many things have changed since the original publication of The Princess Diaries series, most things have stayed the same:

Struggling to pass Algebra. Fighting — and making up — with your best friend. Getting asked out by the boy you secretly like. Being forced to have dinner with your grandmother. Cats. Foreign princes attempting to overthrow the throne. High-school graduation. And real princesses!

I hope you'll accept my royal invitation to visit Genovia (and the world of The Princess Diaries). I just know you're going to enjoy the trip.

Much love

Meg

Books by Meg Cabot

The Princess Diaries series
1. The Princess Diaries
2. A Royal Disaster
3. Princess in the Middle
4. Royally Obsessed
5. Prom Princess
6. Royal Rebel
7. Party Princess
8. Royal Scandal
9. Bad Heir Day
10. Crowning Glory
11. Royal Wedding (*for older readers*)

The Abandon series
The Airhead series
The Mediator series
All-American Girl
All-American Girl: Ready or Not
Avalon High
How to Be Popular
Jinx
Teen Idol
Tommy Sullivan Is a Freak

For younger readers
The Allie Finkle's Rules for Girls series
The Notebooks of a Middle-School Princess series

MEG CABOT

THE PRINCESS DIARIES

MACMILLAN

First published in the UK 2001 by Macmillan Children's Books

This edition published 2015 by Macmillan Children's Books
an imprint of Pan Macmillan
20 New Wharf Road, London N1 9RR
Associated companies throughout the world
www.panmacmillan.com

ISBN 978-1-4472-8062-0

5 7 9 8 6

A CIP catalogue record for this book is available from the British Library.

Typeset by Nigel Hazle
Printed and bound by CPI Group (UK) Ltd, Croydon CR0 4YY